4-85

**A Tale of Devastating Intimacy Between a Lonely Man
and the Daughter He Does Not Know How to Love**

IF I SHOULD DIE BEFORE I WAKE

**A Journey into a World of Imagination and Poetic Beauty,
Incomprehensible Brutality and Heartstopping Suspense**

"Stunning and brilliant . . . astonishing power . . . unerring suspense . . . unforgettable."—*San Francisco Chronicle*

"What might have been sensationalistic material is handled with deep feeling and insight—a horrifying and heartrending novel."—*Publishers Weekly*

"A shocking child's-eye view of sexual abuse . . . a stunning statement."—*Library Journal*

"The most powerful item yet in the social movement of eradication of sexual abuse of children."
—Roland Summit, M.D., Los Angeles County Chairperson,
   The Child Sexual Abuse Project Advisory Committee

"A very moving experience. I recommend it highly."
   —Dr. Henry Giaretto,
      Founder and Director of Parents United

"Carla is one of the most remarkable heroines in modern fiction. . . . *If I Shou . . . . . . fore I Wake* [is] perhaps the best and most impor . . . . *. . . urant*

If I Should Die Before I Wake

Michelle Morris

A DELL BOOK

Published by
Dell Publishing Co., Inc.
1 Dag Hammarskjold Plaza
New York, New York 10017

To Larry,
my beloved husband—
fidens et constans.
To our son David,
who brings us joy.
And to all the Carlas.

Many thanks to the J. P. Tarcher staff for giving so much to this book. And the author most gratefully acknowledges the loyal support of her family, especially Larry and David, Gail Shoden, Marguerite Kerin, Katherine Morris, and David Gilmore; and friends whose love sustains beyond measure: Steve and Marilyn Golden, Laura Grau, Louise Jurgens, Leslie Stevenson, and Wendy Whitaker.

"Some are born to deep delight.
Some are born to endless night."

WILLIAM BLAKE

If I Should Die
Before I Wake

One

***

*N*OW I'M READY.

My hands are tight around the heavy police revolver you take so much pride in. My forefingers stroke the trigger.

Your body is curled up all innocent like a giant baby's on the king-sized bed. The dark blue top sheet is twisted underneath your arm and shoulder and one of the pillows is stuffed between your drawn-up knees and your big head is down flat because you don't like a pillow there. I know. Because I know all your traits and habits, don't I? Like how you came to be in this deep sleep tonight and how you'll stay this way long into tomorrow.

If I let you.

I won't, of course. When I'm ready to finish this, I will awaken you and engage your full attention. But first I want to savor being here in your overstuffed bedroom chair, watching you sleep trustingly as a puppy while I balance your gun on my knees. There is time, after all. I need only raise my arms a precise number of inches when the moment comes.

Did I remember to thank you for teaching me how to shoot? What a clean unswerving word that is—shoot. Or have you forgotten those Saturday afternoons when you'd drive me out to the range to practice with you? It was good for me, you'd say. In case of an intruder. If I needed to defend myself while you were away. Yes. How you've always loved the ironic. The macabre. And, naturally, how confident you are.

My palms are tingling and wet around the handle of the gun, so I make myself loosen them. There is no need for hurry. The important thing, as I cherish this fine unfailing hardness in my hands, is that I'm in control now. And for the first time since I can remember, I am breathing from way down inside.

You are breathing, too, deeply and serenely, as you lie there; even your slumber is cocksure. And in your arrogance when you awaken, you will smile. No matter the gun in my hands. In that ugly, careless way of yours, you will be laughing at me, entertained by my resolve, by my ludicrous sense of purpose.

Yes, your retaliation will be that smile, familiar to me as the morning sun and, by your own appraisal, your most profitable asset. You will expect that smile, with its touch of bewildered and friendly supplication, to call my bluff. You will count on that guileless light in your eyes to undo me.

But such a ploy can only succeed when your opponent is also bluffing.

And I am not.

At last I have come to rest inside my own vision.

But in the beginning was the word, your word, my father. Impalpable as air and, for me, as necessary. Yet quite meaningless to you.

And it will soon be over. When we no longer care, they
will find us here in this strange silent house—a mad dog
lying in the darkness of his own blood. And me.
    When it is over.
    When the seal is broken.

Dear Ms. Silva—Jessica—Jessie: you burst into my life
this morning like a clap of magnificent thunder! From the
moment I saw you I could feel it coming on, an enchant-
ment to bring color and hope back into my life.

And I'm not even sure yet why I'm so drawn to you.
Could it be the loveliness of your face? Or perhaps the
compassion in it? You are more than beautiful. My memory of how you look—soft auburn hair curling down
around your neck, your tawny complexion, the doelike
grace of your movements—that memory is indelible.

And your eyes, those dark eyes that say everything.

Of course, we'll never see each other again.

I doubt you've seen me at all, at least not to remember.
This morning I was just a face among forty-some kids in
social science, and during the discussion after your talk, I
didn't say a word.

I guess I wasn't even listening.

Preoccupied instead with writing down your name and
telephone number—over and over again.

A twenty-four-hour hotline number you're inviting us
to call. Let me say at once that I can imagine nothing
more soothing for a crisis than the sound of your voice.
And the way your accent gives every word you say a kind
of languor.

Yes. I sat there adoring you, safe in the knowledge that
you would never notice me. Not the skinny sexless kid
with circles under her eyes and the atrocious posture who
sits at the back of the class.

11

Oh, Jessie.

What if I would call you tonight?

Yet I'm afraid of everything. I want to reach out to you, but first I must build my courage. Until I do, I will probably be like Hamlet, agonizing my life away. And writing you unsendable letters like this one.

This whole morning I've been lost in daydreams about you and me. Since I already crave the sound of your laughter, I want to tell you jokes. I don't know any clean ones, so I plan to get a book of them out of the library. I even imagine us sharing poetry together and enjoying silences rich with meaning.

And, in my most daring moments, I actually see myself curled up like a child in the dark, your voice a soft hand on my forehead as you sing me to sleep.

Mama—come sing to me.

Please, Mama, it's dark and the face of the nightmonster comes in my eyes. The face is big and wet and there are dark smells all around me. And after a while the fastness always comes, the moving of the fastness, and it gets louder to me and then it stops for a little minute and then most of the hurting, most of the burn part comes 'cause it's so fast now and it goes sharp like that and then it stops and comes apart and then it quietens so much, like it's all gone, and it's still as can be. Then comes the heavy part and pretty soon it's heavy all over me and pushing down on me all over and I can't get air in me and I can't get air out of me and it gets black in my head and the shiny things come in my eyes and the bigness leaves off and then I can get air again and the burn part comes back real sharp now and gets sharper and I try to move but I don't feel anything, only the burn part. I bite me real hard to make the burn part go away, and then it gets all black.

12

Oh, Mama—I wait for you so long.
Why don't you come?

It's been just four hours, Jessie, and I'm already afraid of you. If we're ever to talk to each other, you'll want to know who I am. You will not want to hear jokes or sing songs or play silly games with me. You will expect me to have something serious to work on. And I can see us now—two surgeons at an operating table huddled over my problem.

But just the thought of you loosens my tongue (or my pen) in the most dangerous way. Jessie—you are as seductive to me as the bosom of a loving mother. And I haven't had a mother since I was five years old.

No. There can be no revelations, so there can be no you.

Because I am not the shy girl of almost seventeen that you imagine me to be.

I am bitter. I am isolated. I seethe with passions of the wrong kind.

I am a whited sepulchre filled with dead men's bones.

An evil stench and you'd be forced to turn away.

It's nearly five-thirty. I must have slept.

Sometimes I doze off this way, sitting here by the bedroom window in my rocking chair, an old quilt wrapped around my knees.

The window is open, and I'm looking up into a sky made radiantly pure by this morning's winds. The air is still now, and the late afternoon sun wraps its soft arms around me.

I love the sun.

It has the power to cleanse, and make new.

And to protect.

I felt it today in the library. The sun coming in through the narrow churchlike windows and warming the volumes all around me. I closed my eyes and let myself be filled with this tranquility.

I was looking so stupid that Mrs. Burnett came to ask if anything was wrong. Embarrassing. And frightening, too. Because I can feel it now. The scent of this danger comes to me by instinct, as it does to an animal.

Change.

When it takes all the energy I possess to keep things the same.

And the change is in him, too. In my father. I could tell by the message waiting for me on the kitchen blackboard when I came home. The one that says he'll be working late tonight and won't want dinner till eight-thirty. Violent upturns in his handwriting tell me that some strong emotion is driving him today.

A disquieting thought.

I couldn't indulge it for long, though, because there were things to do. The laundry. Dinner to be made. Promises to keep. And miles and miles to go . . . .

First, the sheets on my father's big bed. I pulled them off the mattress and bundled them up; then I dragged them downstairs, holding on by just the corners. Later I made the tuna casserole. But I couldn't concentrate, and I think I may have left something out, or put something in twice.

I'm not sure.

Afterwards I walked around our new house, but not really looking at anything because there is no need to become involved here. It is just another neglected place my father and I will strive to make beautiful—then sell at a profit that is just as handsome. We have been here three weeks now, so the work will begin very soon.

I could sleep again, I think.

I feel old.

What is worse—I can feel something trying to work its way out of the darkness inside my brain.

And I am afraid to close my eyes.

Mama, when I'm asleep the nightmonster comes to me and air goes all out of me and makes me feel dead. Then I wake up and he's gone, only I'm still scared, Mama, and I go to your room, but you aren't there anymore and it's the real nightmonster. He pulls me in bed and says, what pretty hair, all soft, and he plays with my hair and then he holds me too tight and says, my little Goldilocks, and his mouth has a bad dark smell. It gets dark all around me then and the fastness comes again and I can't scream.

I finished my chores, and now I'm lying on the floor next to the bed.

They are here, too—I can feel them.

My dear companions.

Leona Ly: Hush, little ones. Hush now.
Mymouse: Leona Ly? Where are you?
Leona Ly: Right here. Yes—that's it. I'll rock you to sleep.
Punkey: Look, I'll smack him this time! Just watch me! I will!
Leona Ly: No, Punkey, not now. Sh-h-h.
Kristal: Oh, I must take a shower—a scalding hot shower—for an hour and an hour.

Dear Kristal—yes. I will make myself clean again. I will burn myself clean.

15

I feel better now, Jessie. I stayed in the shower for a long time, till the water went cold.

Kristal always knows the best thing to do.

I've been fooling my father. He thinks Kristal and the others are just puppets. That the Upside Down Theatre is something I use to entertain, and nothing more.

For I'm a puppeteer. And until I heard your voice this morning, my favorite sound in the world was the laughter of little children. When I perform, it washes over me like the moving silver sound of a waterfall. I look out from my stage at the kids and their enthralled faces, and I drink in that laughter, so full of excitement and affection, and relief when the dangers have passed.

But the soft bodies that seem to live on my hands are only disguises. Illusions, you might say.

My puppets are actually Voices. And they are real.

The youngest of the children always know this. That's why they sometimes wander up to the stage and talk to my Voices themselves.

So I'm sure you'll understand that what I live for is to do this thing I love most: to create an enchanted place, a separate and mystical world, for little kids and me.

And now there is you. These letters.

Perhaps you're wondering why I write to you, Jessie. And why I don't destroy these letters after I finish them.

It's just that there seem to be things I have to say, and the idea of saying them to myself is too bizarre.

I don't throw these letters away because I find myself wanting to read them again and again. I even enjoy the feel of them in my hands. In some uncanny way, they prove there really is a Carla Jean Hughes.

At least they prove it to me.

I do wonder sometimes. I even wonder what I look like because I honestly don't know. Like a vampire, I find no reflection in my mirror.

Other people's opinions don't help that much either. For instance, my father tells me that my complexion has all the color of a newly peeled potato, while Dean says that my skin is like sweet cream. My father insists that I look as emaciated as the victim of a concentration camp, but Dean calls me his pixie, and says the gamin look is the true me.

Yes, Dean.

My friend.

Only I'm not ready to tell you about him yet.

Right now I feel the need to confess to you that despite Dean's generous appraisal, I am often mistaken for a boy. Because what "curves" I have are subtle to the point of nonexistence. In fact, the very thought of being female take me right to the brink of nausea.

Which doesn't stop my father from buying me clothes that are absurdly feminine—things, by the way, that I wear as seldom as humanly possible. Dad says the clothing I choose looks like it comes from the Salvation Army, and actually, most of it does. When Dad and I go to their thrift shop for furniture to refinish, I always swipe an item of apparel when he isn't looking. Like my favorite blouse, the one with mustard yellow stripes on a background of purple, the colors my father hates most.

I know what you're thinking, Jessie. You can't imagine anything more inhumane than shoplifting from the Salvation Army. But it really is okay, because afterward I always send them a generous donation.

I do have a little money, you see. I keep it right here on my desk in the onyx box my father gave me last Christmas. It's the money I earn when I let my Voices reveal themselves to children.

But, as you now know, those are not the only times my dear companions speak. For my Voices live in the sheltering darkness under the bed, and every night I sleep on the floor beside them.

17

Right by the bed. No—I will not shrink from telling you about it, but if you need to know this, Jessie, you will have to brace yourself. Because the bed in my room is surpassingly weird. Something right out of William Faulkner or Edgar Allan Poe.

And the kind of stories in which time has stood still.

My room is dominated by a little girl's dream of a four-poster canopy bed. With a pink organdy coverlet and a matching canopy overhead. My father purchased this monstrosity for me when I was eight. It is a fitting irony that the bed has endured all these years precisely because of my refusal to sleep in it.

When I look at this bed, I can hear myself screaming inside. It makes me think of China and the binding of little girl's feet. I am too old for this bed, and everything about it disgusts me. I have to say it again, Jessie—I do not sleep in this grotesqueness. Not ever.

I sleep next to it on top of my sleeping bag—not inside the bag because that would be much too confining. And when the nights are cool I wrap myself in my old quilt, a warm flannel one I found at the Salvation Army. During the long watchful hours I reach under the bed for the things I cherish.

Notes from dying kids in a hospital where I performed once.

A seashell and letter Dean gave me on the best day of my life.

And a gray dog-eared volume as dear to me as the Bible—containing every poem ever written by Emily Dickinson.

I need to tell you about Emily.

I love her like a sister even though she's been dead for years and years. Because she understands me better than anyone else ever has.

Her words are still living, trapped inside her books. Trapped the way she was, buried alive in a house where people actually believe she stayed of her own free will.

My eleventh-grade English teacher said that nobody knows why Emily never left her first home, that this is an enigma in literature. After all her poems were published and the scholars had studied them, not even they saw the truth.

Only how can that be? When *I* know. Remember when Emily says:

> *A great Hope fell*
> *You heard no noise*
> *The Ruin was within*
> *Oh cunning wreck that told no tale*
> *And let no Witness in. . . .*

Now what could be more clear? Isn't it obvious that she was afraid someone would read this while she was still alive? Would guess her secret?

And that would have destroyed her world.

So she kept her poems hidden in a box, maybe even under a canopy bed, for someone like me to find.

Oh, Jessie, now do you see?

In spite of everything, Emily never forgot her destiny. She found a way to be a poet.

And when a poet dies, yet still lives—if she keeps her pact with the truth.

Emily did.

Even though she was his:

> *He put the Belt around my life—*
> *I heard the Buckle snap*
> *And turned away, imperial,*
> *My Lifetime folding up. . . .*

* * *

He will be here in an hour.

I wait for my father as the afternoon light slowly dies.

And I am beset by memories.

Dean.

A prism of recollections putting his face before me in a thousand ways.

I think it is time now to tell you about him.

Above all, Jessie, he has dignity.

It was the first thing I saw in him before I saw anything else, nearly one year ago on the day we officially met. At the beginning of my first and only year at Alvarado High. All I knew about Dean Lowrey was that he wrote for the school newspaper and we had world history together. But until that day we had never spoken.

Dean and I owe our relationship to the cold-bloodedness of our peers. Just before the first dance of the school year, the junior class "in"group decided to play a joke on Dean Lowrey and me. People I thought were trying to be friendly kept telling me that Dean wanted to meet me and ask me to the dance. Naturally Dean was getting a similar story about my reported attraction to him. Only later did I find out why we two were selected for this scenario— that Dean and I were considered "untouchables" by the entire junior class.

On the morning of the dance I was told to meet Dean at my locker between first and second period. I was terrified because my father doesn't allow me any outside associations and fascinated because it was the first time anyone my age had ever seemed interested in me.

The next thing I knew, Dean was standing there, just observing me in that patient, searching way of his. I would like to describe him to you, but the stark physical facts will not begin to do him justice. For one thing, Dean lacks All-American macho appeal because he is small for his age, not much taller than I am and no more than ten or twelve pounds heavier. His eyes are a lot like yours, Jessie, big and wonderfully expressive and velvet dark. His face has an aristocratic look, not unlike that of the poet, John Donne. Oh—and the minute you see his thick, silky black hair, your fingertips positively yearn to touch it.

Anyway, Dean stood beside me that day with the jaunty posture I've come to think of as his "Mighty Mouse" look, and then came the sensation of a group beginning to materialize around us. It was clear from the expectant looks and hushed asides that our classmates were waiting for a show.

Immobilized by my humiliation, I took refuge in Dean's brown eyes. He was leaning casually against the locker next to mine and looking utterly at ease. He even appeared to be enjoying himself, like an actor playing a scene, treating the audience as part of the natural order of things.

For one appalling moment, I thought that Dean himself was part of this plot, that he and the crowd were coconspirators out to shame me. Then he was smiling what can only be called an affectionate smile—at me. The crowd sounds faded, and people began to watch us more intently. Dean moved closer to me then and whispered, "Do what I tell you. Smile and say yes so they all can hear."

For want of a better plan and because I am so accustomed to taking orders, I said yes. I even managed something like a smile.

But when Dean slipped his arm around me for a moment, I froze, and when he kissed me on the cheek, my vulnerable face turned crimson. Even though I could not ignore a certain unsettling pleasure in this contact, and the good smell and feel of his skin.

Then he was walking away from me down the hall, head high, the rest of his body loose and easy.

"Shit—he really does like her," a girl whose name I didn't know spoke, her voice petulant with disappointment.

One of the guys snorted. "Oh, yes, dah-ling, of course, he does." He undulated down the hall after Dean.

As I rummaged unnecessarily through my locker, there were other comments, but the ripples of half-hearted laughter soon died away. The joke had been clearly and frustratingly aborted.

The bell rang at last, and I headed for the gym, absorbed now in total admiration for Dean.

Do you know what I mean, Jessie? As my father would put it—class.

In the days that followed, I would catch him looking at me sometimes. But whenever he was near, I scurried away as predictably as a startled mouse.

Until a week later, when Dean came to me during lunch hour. He must have searched long and hard for me, too, because I was sitting alone in a grassy secluded place I'd found behind the school auditorium.

The moment I saw him, my pathological shyness took over; my throat closed against any possibility of speech. And guilt was already twitching between by shoulder blades because I was viewing this scene through my father's eyes—my father, who'd be sure to think I had encouraged Dean to come here.

After he joined me on the ground nearby, Dean moved his pale fingers lightly over the blades of grass that lay between us. "Hi," he said.

Avoiding his eyes, I could only nod.

His hands drifted upward, clasping over his fine black hair, and anchoring softly together on his head. "Uh, I'm sorry about those kids the other day."

Struck by the injustice of his making this apology, I shook my head.

He returned his delicate fingers to the thick cool grass. "You just have to ignore that whole group."

Feeling like a fool, I nodded again.

"Anyway, I hope I didn't upset you or anything. But I thought we handled it okay."

"*You* did," I heard myself say.

His sudden smile warmed me. "No. Not without you, Carla."

My name. And the way he said it—dreamily, caressingly, so that it seemed no longer mine. As though it had gained somehow in worth and stature. And was strangely evocative of a time long ago. The way a woman might have said it perhaps. An exquisitely gentle woman.

When I didn't speak, Dean gave me another of the penetrating looks I would come to know so well. "You do know why they did it."

I shook my head again.

With an air of resolve, he drew his legs up smoothly into the lotus position and wrapped his fingers around his slender ankles. "I guess you know it's me."

Surprised by this change in his mood, I was reminded of my father.

"They feel like they've got me all figured out." His jaw locked tight for a moment as he studied me. "They just think I'm weird, you know?"

My shyness became a haze dissolved by the sun. I could even picture myself moving over and taking Dean into my arms the way I do Mymouse sometimes, ready to offer him all the compassion I possess.

Tears hung frozen in his eyes. "Not what guys are supposed to be anyway."

His honesty stung me, and too late did my hands cover my renegade mouth. "But you're beautiful."

"Right." He closed his eyes for a moment. "Only I

think that's the wrong adjective, don't you? But thanks anyway."

I wanted to disappear.

After a long pause he spoke again, his tone embittered now. "My grandmother always used to say things like that about me. Like how my eyelashes were 'much too marvelous' to waste on a boy."

Then, in one swift, nimble movement, he was on his feet, brushing off his clothing, though not one blade of grass had dared cling to it. "Well—I have to go."

I watched him walk away from me, and even this he accomplished with a dancer's silent grace.

That last image of him stayed with me for the rest of the day, and on into the long despairing hours of the night.

The casserole is in the oven.

And the sky is melancholy now. Soon darkness will spread over everything, like a giant's shadow.

I can't stop thinking about Dean.

How he came back the next day and was waiting for me at noon at my "secret" place. Stretched out comfortably on the grass, leaning on one elbow, his other arm languid on his hip.

He greeted me as cheerfully as though there had been no misunderstanding. "Hey—about yesterday," he added. "I was dumb."

I felt inordinate relief.

He motioned to the grass beside him. "Sit down, okay?"

I obeyed.

"Yeah, so I'm sorry. The way I walked off and all. I'm just too damn sensitive, you know?"

Yes, I thought. I know.

"Anyway, I never even told you yesterday what I wanted to tell you." He took an orange out of his lunch sack and thrust half of it toward me. "What I wanted to say is I was already planning to talk to you. I mean, before that whole thing happened with those kids."

Embarrassed by this effort to salvage our feelings, I searched for words to stop him.

"I mean it, Carla. I was."

"It doesn't matter."

"No—hey. You don't believe me, do you? But I've seen you before. I mean, before school started."

My discomfort deepened into fear.

He seemed to be reading my expression. "Don't worry. It was just over at the library. Last summer. I was there with my little brothers. You gave that puppet show, remember?"

Feeling as though my privacy had been somehow invaded, I pulled up a handful of grass and cast it away from me. "Oh."

He was smiling. "The one I liked best was—uh—Punkey. The monkey. He was great. I have trouble with my temper sometimes, too. But I guess you already know. From yesterday."

Too harsh a judgment, I thought.

"Anyway, that theatre of yours is fantastic, Carla. And I just wanted to tell you myself." He wiped his fingers on a napkin. "The guys loved you, too."

"Who?"

"You know—the little guys. Eric and Derrick. My foster brothers."

"Your family has foster kids?"

"You could say that." He grimaced. "I feel so sorry for the twins. Stuck with those awful rhyming names and everything." But the warmth in his eyes made me envy them.

"So I really did want to meet you. When those creeps started everything, it gave me the perfect way."

"You knew?" I blurted out.

He raised one black eyebrow. "Suspected. But it isn't exactly the first time, you know. For me."

"It wasn't just you, though."

He looked away from me, as if he knew eye contact then would be too intimate. "I know."

And then I said something else, what I'd planned to say if I ever got the chance to talk to Dean again. "They were laughing at me."

"Okay," he said softly. He was looking at the ground.

"I mean, for one thing . . ." I struggled for words. "Well, I walk heavy."

"Huh?"

"That's what my father says. That I walk like a truck driver."

Dean grinned. "You don't look like a truck driver, though."

I went on recklessly. "I don't look like a girl."

He took a candy bar out of his pocket. "'Cause you're a little thin, that's all." He divided the candy and handed half to me. "Eat up."

Then I laughed. Me, Jessie! I actually laughed out loud. I even took the candy bar. I also noticed that I'd finished the orange. "So anyway, I'm the freak," I said. Only now I could feel my chin tremble a little and a thickening in my throat. "Not you, Dean."

He folded the candy wrapper neatly and put it into his pocket. Then he leaned forward, and his finely formed hand nearly touched my bony, squarish one. "You're no freak," he said, looking directly into my eyes, his face very close to mine. "I've watched you for weeks and you're just shy, that's all. In a world of your own."

Having always imagined myself to be invisible, I was stupefied by this revelation.

"Look," he went on, "I'm a loner, too, okay? And maybe . . ."

Waiting for him to finish, I was suddenly eager and afraid.

". . . well, you know. We could be friends maybe. Loners together. If you want."

Friends. Until that moment I had never noticed that word before, how soft and inviting it is. And there was something else happening, too. A memory from when I was little. Of another boy—a boy who was almost my brother.

"All right?" Dean asked.

I thought of my father's disapproval, but my traitorous head nodded yes.

He touched my hand, my hideous, abhorrently damp and shaky hand. "I guess we have to be honest with each other then. Like, well, I could start it off. Because I think you might have the wrong impression about something."

"I do?"

"Yeah. You know. When you asked me about my family before. My little brothers. See—they're real. I mean, they're the real brothers."

"What?"

"Yeah. You know. The foster kid is me."

I didn't say anything.

"Just to be honest about stuff." Dean was looking more relaxed again. "Nothing else seems to work."

And there it was, right from the beginning. Dean's obsession with the truth. A thing that you and I know can be devastating. Can make the very ground shudder beneath your feet.

Despite everything, I made a covenant with him that afternoon. The yearning part of me agreed in the face of it all. And for a long time I didn't remember anything else about what happened afterward. Not the bell ringing or our walking together back toward the main building. Or when Dean got the idea about putting on another show for the kids and put his arm around me while we walked, his forearm dangling down over my shoulder in that casual way you always see with high school kids on campus.

Only it had never been me before. Not with the warm protective weight of someone's arm around me.

And it was only the beginning.

Sometimes now, when I'm lying alone in the dark and I let myself comprehend that Dean and I are so far apart, I wonder if I will sink into this blackness forever. Then I try to remember everything that has happened between us and I bring him back to me. I stroke his silky black hair and guide my fingers to his lips and tell myself that he is here.

But it's a lie, Jessie. I can't touch my friend anymore. My loving friend. My love.

And sometimes that is like death.

In spite of all that's happened, I haven't forgotten that the sun set beautifully tonight—an Almost Perfect Thing—the mother-of-pearl sky lit from within by a dying sun, the clouds edged with gold, and over everything a pale blue as pure as the color of my father's eyes.

I saw it from the kitchen as I finished making dinner.

And when I looked out into the quiet street at the imposing house across from ours, I felt that wonder again at how far we've come in the last twelve years. How far we've come in terms of what counts with my father— houses, property, what he calls the "golden promise" of California real estate.

28

If only it would bring him peace.

When I'd finished making the salad, I looked at the blackboard to see how my father had addressed me in his message. Because each of his names for me has a meaning all its own. And I keep track of his moods with unrelenting vigilance, the way a life-support system monitors a dying patient.

This afternoon's note had no salutation, which meant my father was probably in a hurry, but haste alone could not explain the distortion of his handwriting. I knew there was something more.

So I set the dining room table with special care. We always eat rather formally, my father and I, using the silver I keep so impeccably polished, Waterford crystal goblets, and the most fragile china.

And tonight a yellow rose.

I had watched this flower grow, framed by our kitchen window, for nearly a week—and it was just beginning to open. Tonight when I went to cut it down, I breathed in its incomparable perfume, and your name, Jessie, drifted into my mind once again. I touched my lips for a moment to its velvety petals, and those petals reminded me of the soft dusky skin of your face.

I put the rose into a crystal bud vase, positioning it near my father's place at the head of the dining room table. The rose would please him, I knew, might even be crucial to his frame of mind tonight. He hasn't had time to plant his own flowers at this new house, and I sometimes think the only thing in the world he truly loves is his garden.

I heard the brief buzz of the garage door opener, checked the table one last time, and went back into the kitchen to greet him. I listened to the way he closed the car door, the sound and tempo of his footsteps, and how he opened the connecting door into the kitchen. Tonight there was a briskness to all those sounds, and soon he was standing before me, the fresh smell of the outdoors about him, his broad, flushed face radiating pride.

"Carla! I did it!"

I handed him an open can of beer. "What, Dad?"

He lifted the can to his mouth for a second, then actually lowered it without drinking. "That Johnstone property, remember? The one that needed everything—new plumbing, the works. Johnstone priced it right out of the market. Which isn't hard these days since there isn't any fucking market. Anyway, baby, I sold it!"

My father took a deep swig of the beer and then another. He looked like a big blond bear, pleased as a kid with an all "A" report card. As I moved about the kitchen, he kept beaming his smile at me; I could feel it on my back as I took the tuna casserole out of the oven.

"All day I just knew it in my bones. Couple called the Holts bought it. Didn't blink an eye over the financing either. Last of the big-time spenders."

At that moment I was scrutinizing a watery-looking and slightly gray tuna casserole, sure now I'd made some crucial error in the recipe. And hoping my father's exhilaration would sustain him through yet another of my questionable dinners.

"So I caught the boss on the way out and told him. You should have seen his face. Remember how he acted when he first hired me? You know—said I had a reputation to overcome. Do you believe that? I had a reputation all right. Seven straight months as top salesman at Global. But the boss could care less about that. Said if I didn't play by the rules he'd cut my balls off."

It was easy to see that my father was tuning up for a monologue. Whenever he's happy or excited about something, he talks nonstop, kind of a chatter really. It isn't necessary to reply or anything—or even to listen. I usually just go on with whatever I'm doing.

"I felt like telling him, 'This is a business, Lloyd, not a goddamned tea party.' He isn't like *one* of the other small businessmen I know. Thinks he can cross every *t* just so and still make it, and in this economy yet. Fat chance!"

After his last long drink of beer, my father opened the refrigerator and took out a half-filled bottle of wine. "I'm propping up the whole office at this point, Carly. I was their number one salesman all summer, and that's exactly how it's going to stay. Sure, problems develop with my deals sometimes. But that's the name of the game—risk. I get stuck with a lot of the problem properties in that office because nobody else can handle them. And problem properties breed problem deals."

I finished bringing everything into the dining room, and Dad seated himself like a potentate at the end of the long oval table. "I can't wait till Ms. Mimi Harrison hears about this. Before I came, she was the big deal over there. But she and those other bitches have real respect for me now. When they hear about this Johnstone thing, they'll all be in line to kiss my ass."

I am moved to apologize for my father's way of expressing himself, as well as for my unabridged presentation of it. I tried leaving blanks where the profanity is, but that doesn't seem to work. My father uses so many four-letter words that when I censor them, most of his sentences just collapse.

But I do detest those words. And I detest even more the way he uses them, especially sitting at the dining room table with silver and flickering candles and a perfect yellow rose. Sometimes when I'm watching him speak, I imagine that his words are bits of mud plopping out onto our snow-white linen tablecloth.

His mouth full of casserole now, Dad was frowning at me. "Hey, this shit is the worst, girl." He pushed his plate away. "We're supposed to be celebrating tonight, and here we are eating crap like this." He drained his wine-glass. Then, with a touch of sadness and resignation, he reached over to spear another bite of the execrable dinner. "Why do you do this to me?"

A rhetorical question, to be sure. And the reason I do it is that I can't cook. Even after years of practice, I never seem to be able to keep my mind on it. At least I think that's the explanation. Dean says that I don't want to cook and this is an expression of rebellious hostility toward my father. Dean was in therapy for two and a half years, which gives him a tendency to analyze everything. I've told him there isn't a shred of truth to his theory, but he just arches one eyebrow and smiles that exasperating smile of his. I've decided never to reveal the strange "gourmet" touches I purposely add to my father's food sometimes. Dean is enough of a know-it-all as it is.

With a final look of disgust, my father laid down his fork and refilled his crystal goblet with wine. Then he lifted the glass to his lips with what can only be described as reverent affection. "Of course, selling is what I've always been best at, Carly. Even when I was a kid. I was the one who always sold the most chocolate bars and newspaper subscriptions. After that big drive when I was a senior in high school, Father Snyder even mentioned my name to the bishop. But was my old man impressed? Hell, no. He was always just plain down on selling. And here I am now making ten times the money he ever did—even after he made captain in the fire department. I'd sure like him to see me now. And this new place we've got. It'd knock his eyes out."

Have I mentioned that my father hasn't spoken to his parents for twelve years? Or his brother or sister? Dad says they don't even know where we are anymore, and he doesn't care because he never could stand them anyway.

He picked up the wine bottle again and poured out

what was left; I could see the maroon liquid rising eerily in his goblet like blood. "I'm damn good at what I do, kid, and it's a far cry from being a fireman or a cop. Even if they're the only careers my old man could ever see. Not satisfied unless I got burned to death or my head blown off or something. 'Manly,' he always called it. 'The manly thing.' Well, I tried the cops, Carly, like I told you, and it's strictly for losers. Those guys have no fucking futures at all. They just collect human garbage."

Yes, I'd heard this before, many times.

'. . . dead, baby."

"What?"

Dad was staring at the empty wine bottle as though it had betrayed him. "This one's dead. What else is there?"

"The burgundy." I stood up. "Or the chablis."

"Either one."

When I came back with the burgundy, I could see that my father's eyes, glistening unexpectedly in the candlelight, were focused at last on the yellow rose.

"Nice," he said gently. "Get it from the yard?"

I nodded.

"That's good, baby." He reached out to touch the flower, his fingertips grazing its petals tenderly. "It's like you knew we'd be celebrating tonight." He grasped the bud vase, his blue eyes misty now. "It's this thing between the two of us. Like telepathy or something. The way we always know what's going on with each other."

I was the watching the rose. "We'll have *your* flowers soon."

He leaned forward heavily. Then he smiled the broad sentimental smile that sometimes comes in this stage of his drinking. "I already do."

I looked down at my plate.

"I have you," he said. He turned to the wine bottle I'd brought him and cleared his throat. Then he poured himself another glass, raising it to me in a kind of toast. "My little flower."

Oh, Daddy.

I lifted my water glass. "Success, Dad."

He grinned and repeated, with a sigh of satisfaction, "Success." He drank deeply, then wiped his eyes with the back of one big hand. "Oh, I tell you, baby. It's all going to happen for us. We're going to do it this time. Get this place done and buy that dream house we've always wanted in the Palisades. A house built right out on a cliff, over the water. With the best view in the whole god-damned area."

"Oh, no—we can't move again!"

His smooth, pale face clouded over. "Jesus, girl, with interest rates like they are, it'll take a few more months anyhow. The real estate business is practically dead at this point. And we'll have to get this place all ready."

His words were starting to wind down, like a recording losing power, and I warned myself to be careful.

"Just don't you worry about a thing, kid. You can still finish your senior year here. But remember—we didn't do all this moving to stop now. That house at the beach is our goal. We're going to have a permanent place to live this time. A place the whole world will envy. And no smog."

I know what you're thinking, Jessie, but I'm not stupid either, at least not about some things. And I know my father is never going to find a house or a neighborhood that truly satisfies him.

And of course it never occurs to him that I could have dreams of my own.

Then he was eyeing me shrewdly. "Unless you think that turning seventeen Monday is going to change any-thing for you. Don't fool yourself, Carla. You're still go-ing to be the same shy kid. Scared to death of other people. Scared to drive a car or even go to the market by yourself. You're still going to live with me and be taken care of. And don't think I mind it, baby. No way. That's exactly what a father is for."

This subject has been a mine field between Dad and me for about a year now. As casually as I could, I said, "But what if I would go away to college next September." I said this with some assurance, even though the idea is frightening to me.

His face hardened with impatience. "Oh, sure, kid. You say 'away' like it was down the block or something. You don't even know the meaning of the word. And you sure as hell couldn't handle it."

All at once I could hear Dean coaching me from somewhere inside my head: Stay cool, Carla. Try not to argue. Just make your plans. Only I'm not even sure they are my plans. They could be Dean's—his plans for me.

Still, I found myself stirred by another impulse to mutiny. "I can't keep moving around this way, Dad. Nine different places already."

The look on my father's face told me what I should have known all along. I was going too far. And now his expression was menacing. "You counted, huh? After everything I've done for you. After all I've given up. You ungrateful bitch!" He was clutching the wine goblet so tightly I expected it to shatter, could almost see the glass biting savagely into his hands, his blood staining the white tablecloth. "Would you rather have stayed in one of those sleazy dives we started out in? Like that furnished room where the fleas almost ate us alive? Or how 'bout that filthy hole on Crenshaw above the cleaners?"

Recalling that last one, his expression changed to one of malevolent triumph. But I shut out the sudden and unspeakable memory before it could take hold.

"We came here with nothing and don't you ever forget it. Only I hustled, didn't I? I learned real fast about California real estate. And I worked my balls off. You think it was easy getting this far? But what the hell do you know about making a living? Not one goddamned thing. All you are is a mouth to feed."

That isn't so, Jessie. In fact, it's a lie. I've worked harder in my life than most kids ever think of doing, helping Dad with the major remodeling of every place we've ever lived in. "Fixer-uppers" he always calls them. And together we make them right. For other people.

"Well, that's enough." His mouth twisted bitterly. "I'm sick of screwing around here with you. I'm going to get out and do some real celebrating. You're not going to wreck this one for me."

Instantly wary, I came to attention. "I'm sorry, Dad."

He contemplated me for a long moment. Then he gave me a sweetly knowing look. "All right then. Let's go out to the Silver Mine tonight. We can have a drink there with Bucky Hogan."

Bucky is my father's main drinking buddy and only real friend, and he is out at the Silver Mine Saloon every night. Bucky—a generous-hearted man who always buys drinks for other people and winds up with empty pockets at the end of the evening. He's pushing forty, I think, just like my father, but Bucky has this gentlemanly way about him. And I can't imagine him ever hurting anyone.

But the fact is, Jessie, that I hate bars. I stared down into my decomposing food. "Dad, please. I'd rather not."

"Oh, really?" Dad said. "The way you enjoy spending time with our friend Bucky?" There was a leer in his voice now; he was already passing into his mean phase with its uncalled-for wickedness.

So please disregard my father's innuendos. There is certainly nothing like that between Bucky and me. Except that I do like him. And the reason I like him, which I know will sound strange, is because he treats me like a child. I

36

know that isn't what most kids want, but I do. I hardly ever see Bucky really, but when I do he always reminds me to lock the doors after they leave and to keep emergency numbers by the telephone. Little nothing stuff like that.

I took a deep breath. "Sure I like him, Dad. But I just don't feel well tonight." Which was true, since I'm always sickened by the thought of going to the Silver Mine. I wish I could just come right out and tell my father how I feel about that place, with its stale cigarette smoke and pernicious smell of booze. People there are always so much older than I am, and they change as the evening wears on—their eyes glaze over and their mouths slacken, and pretty soon they aren't looking at each other at all.

"You're sick," Dad was saying sardonically. "That's terrific. Mighty convenient, too."

"I—I have cramps."

A jubilant smile lit his face. "You had your period two weeks ago. Try again."

Correction: I *pretended* to have my period two weeks ago. I haven't really had my period in nearly two months. But I keep up the fiction anyway because Dad tends to leave me alone if he thinks I'm in that condition.

"I know, Dad. But I've been kind of irregular lately. Just lately."

"Sure—in the last two minutes. I know. And I know you, girl. How you are when you don't want to do something. I know every goddamn one of your excuses."

"The Silver Mine is for adults," I said in desperation.

A wrong move, clearly. "Don't give me that shit." His expression was stony. When he spoke again he separated each word: "You do just fine with adults." He smiled maliciously. "Just fine."

The comment left me speechless.

Gratified by my shame he leaned back in his chair. "Always so accommodating. Aren't you, girl?"

I could feel myself beginning to dissolve inside. But when I found my voice again, I just said meekly, "All right. I'll go."

Enraged, he stood up. "You'll go? What the fuck do you mean, you'll go? Was there ever any doubt? I didn't ask you, did I? I *told* you." His pale eyes glittered at me from an imperious height.

Then, regaining control of himself, he changed his tactics yet again, and his tone was suddenly cloying. "Look, baby—I know you want to go. Don't you?"

My father asked me this because he believes more than anything else in his own power. And so do I.

"Sure, Dad."

"Say it then."

"I want to go."

He loosened his tie. "Then get this table cleaned up. I'm going to change."

When he walked out of the room, I sat still for a moment, taking a ragged breath or two, staring at the white expanse of tablecloth desecrated by the remains of our dinner. When I was numb again, my computerlike mind began sorting rapidly through the data, a familiar kind of safety check: I will go with him ... he is going to drink no matter where he is ... at the bar I will at least be fairly safe ... perhaps when we come home he will just pass out ... and then I will be even safer.

Such, Jessie, are the machinations of optimism.

But as I did the dishes, I vowed that I would be watchful, would analyze and evaluate my father's behavior this evening, each facial expression, every change of tone, his body language.

Because sometimes I think of myself as an ornithologist and my father as one of a species of birds of prey. I mean, does the intelligent prey make it its business to understand the vulture? Of course, it does.

As I look over what I have just written, I recognize that the logic of my metaphor is faulty. At first I presented myself as the bird-watcher, the detached observer, but then somehow transformed myself into food for a vulture.

It is illogical, I must admit. But I will let it stand.

I know you're there. Waiting. You want to ask me about this evening. My father and me. You are curious. You need to know. I guess I've even set things up that way.

And yet I'm terribly afraid. You see, the critical thing in my life has always been to hide.

To hide, my dictionary says, is (1) to put or remain out of sight; (2) to conceal for shelter or protection; (3) to keep secret; (4) to turn away in shame or anger.

All of the above, Jessie. I have experienced *to hide* in each of its facets, all its parts. I hide myself: within the walls of this house, among the strangers at school, in each sacred room of the library, and behind my Voices. I remain, as much as it is possible for human flesh to do, out of sight.

To conceal for shelter or protection—yes, that, too. But poorly. Once you have closed your eyes, there is no more shelter or protection. Like Dorothy in the field of poppies, when you go to sleep, it is over. Yet even awake, you are no more than a little caged mouse hurrying futilely hither and yon, inevitably lurching into the four walls that bound your world.

To keep secret. Oh, indeed, Jessie, secrecy is my forte. My ultimate skill. Using guilt for mortar, I have built impenetrable barricades of secrecy.

To turn away in shame or anger. Sometimes I feel I know all there is to know of shame: I am unclean. My leprosy is of the soul. And I must turn away from others—those pure-hearted ones who go on their way, respecting the laws of God and nature.

You accuse me of stalling.

All right then.

Coming upstairs after the dishes are done, I decide to wash my face. I can tell that a pimple has come out on my chin just since dinner. In compliance with the rules of our house, I leave the door of my bathroom open. And I can hear Kristal crying out in frustration:

> What a bore! What a bore!
> A mortal sin to close the door.

I wet a washcloth and press it into my face, then rinse the cloth again in steaming water. But this time when I look up I see him reflected in the mirror. My father, unbuckling his belt and saying offhandedly: "Aren't you going to take a bath?"

"I don't need to."

"Don't you?" I can see his belt dangling at an odd angle from his right hand. With his left hand, he strokes his chin as though checking to see if he needs a shave. "I thought you said you were on your period."

I grasp the edge of the sink. Trying to harden myself, I summon control. For I suddenly yearn to fall down, whimpering piteously, at his feet. To beg him to permit this one symbolic corner of my life—the uses I make of the bathroom—to belong to me. And only to me.

I say nothing.

He is observing me now. "Is that what you're going to wear?"

"Yes, Dad." I look at myself in the mirror to see what I have on—it is the yellow and purple striped blouse from the Salvation Army.

"That outfit stinks, Carla. Wear something else."

"Okay." I turn around to view him full-length in the doorway. He is wearing an undershirt and still has on his suit pants, which his belly strains at the waist. I wonder now why people say my father is handsome. I cannot see that, no matter how hard I try.

His head clears the door frame by only three or four inches. God, I think for the millionth time—he is a giant.

I walk toward him, but his position in the doorway is impassable, and I draw back again. No, I tell myself, the bile rising in my throat. Not game time. Not a game before our night out together. A diversion I am not prepared for to catch me off guard. *No.*

My skin grows icy.

Massaging the belt with his thick fingers, he is looking amused. "Well?"

"What?"

"Aren't you going to change your clothes?"

Steeling myself, I turn back to the mirror. My mind struggles toward possible defenses. Finally I say, "I need to put medicine on my face."

As steady on his feet as if he were sober, he moves into the bathroom and up behind me, his smile innocent and playful. "What's the matter, girl? Pimples?"

I can smell him now, for he is sweating booze. But his intoxication is otherwise hidden, his manner calm and relaxed. Dangerous really. My father's smile becomes a seductive aperture in his face. "You look fine to me."

Our reflections vanish as I open the medicine cabinet and take out the tube of medication. But it slides out of my unstable grasp, clatters against the side of the basin, drops into the water.

Laughing softly, he lays his big hand on my shoulder. "What's the matter, girl?"

"Nothing." I fish the medication out of the basin of steamy water and dry the tube with a towel. The dead weight of his hand follows my moving shoulder. He frowns a little. "That water looks hot," he says. I try to open the tube, but he takes brief hold of my reddened fingers.

And then, as I try once more to open the tube, I can feel his warm breath on my neck, can see the top of his head in the mirror, the dark blond hair brushing my cheek and now both his hands are squeezing my shoulders.

> *Kristal:*   You don't have to feel.
> None of this is real.

"You were bad tonight," my father murmurs into my neck, his lips grazing my skin. "You were a smartmouth, weren't you? And you lied to me about being on your period." The length of his big body presses obscenely into my back and legs. "Now you can make it up to me."

My lips are working before I can make myself speak. "Aren't we going out?"

"Later," he says, his breath heavy and sour, the reek of booze a toxin to my senses. "Maybe this is better after all," he whispers. "Staying home."

No! Not this time!

Fool—that's what you always say!

No. I say no. I have to say no.

The protest dies ignobly inside me.

For now I am suffocating in the tentacles of his embrace. I close my eyes and suck frantically at a place inside my mouth, catch the flesh there between my teeth and bite down hard to tear it, setting the nerves of my cheek on fire, bringing the slow inevitable ooze of blood, the comforting taste of blood to my tongue.

And Kristal chants: Pain is pure. Pain is sure.

Pain is still the only cure.

Pure.

Sure.

Cure.

* * *

42

It's starting to get light.

A window is open, and I can feel the chill of early morning on my face. I'm lying here on the floor wrapped in my quilt, breathing in the memories of the strangers who've used it before me.

My throat hurts far back inside, and the clean slice of pain makes me feel safe again. Nothing more will happen tonight. But I remain awake.

No, I can't go on, Jessie. You're sick with this already.

It's all mucked up now, my dream of the beauty and joy that could happen between us. All mucked up with the hideous, supposedly essential truth.

And I know the question that is stirring inside you. Torturing you, even as it tortures me.

All you want to know is why.

But even if I tell you everything, that question will linger.

Some of the things you said in class are coming back to me. How you and the other hotline monitors really understand "high school women and men." And how our problems can be symptoms. Of deeper underlying problems, you said. Loneliness. Lack of confidence. Unhappy home life.

You think you know, but you don't.

Because it was worse this time. Worse than ever before because I couldn't banish you.

The anesthesia my brain creates for me isn't working now—because of you. Hope. Emily's thing with feathers. You are false, false hope. I wonder why, Jessie. Is it my mistaken dream or your treachery? Treacherous. Traitorous. Disloyal. Unfaithful. Untrue.

The thing with feathers that perches in the soul.

Why couldn't I get numb this time?

You dare to offer hope when there is none.

Get thee away, Jessie. With your false smile and silvery

voice and your promises. Your voice should be registered like a boxer's hands. It has too much power.

As I lie here, candlelight flickers on the knife near my right hand, and the luminous blade torments me with an older than old desire.

For pain is my friend. My one unfaltering friend.

I draw myself up, and my fingers are throbbing with eagerness for the blade.

It is fitting, of course.

Yes, it is.

Because I am filth, just as he says. I am vomit, just as he says. I am excrement, just as he says.

Everything—just as he says.

I'm sorry. I didn't mean to scare you even more. I mean, if you thought I hurt myself. Because it's all right really. I slept about two hours this morning and when I woke up I saw what I had done. It isn't serious at all. Just some letters—three words really—cut into my thigh.

I don't actually remember doing it. Though I do remember wanting to. But that doesn't matter anyway. The first pain is nothing. The good pain comes when you open the cuts again after they've started to heal.

Of course, I know this makes scars. And, yes, I know they're grotesque. But who cares? Do you think I can make myself more unattractive than I already am?

Knives are just toys to me, Jessie. Like words.

But I will make an agreement with you. When I decide to really hurt myself, I'll tell you first. I promise.

What? What did I write on my leg?

Well, it will sound dumb to you. And maybe even a little crazy. But when I look down at my leg, it just says: "I can't scream."

Two

I CAN'T FEEL THE GUN, *my father. It is part of my hands now. And you and I are wrapped in the thinning grayness that comes before dawn. Yes, I am intimate with the moods of the night sky. I keep watch by them and sleep only when the sun is up.*

A gift, one might say, from you. A part of my legacy.

But when the sun rises this morning, neither of us will sleep. When the morning light is full upon us, I will watch that obdurate smile finally disappear from your face. I will see the pristine color of your eyes harden into slate, the Hyde mouth loosen with corruption, erasing Dr. Jekyll's venerable face forever.

Yes, you made a mistake, my father. A fatal error. Even as you built your barricade around me these past twelve years, you left open a narrow fissure in the rock, a single shaft of light to beckon me.

Although your paranoia still devours nearly everything around me, you've seen no danger in the mute passivity of books. You've allowed me to read, and to do so utterly without censorship or discrimination.

The library. Only in that cool, unworldly and tranquil place have I ever been free. Even as my body atrophies from disuse, my mind celebrates itself with this reading. Books feed my soul.

But do I underestimate your cleverness, my father? Did you perhaps calculate this concession to my imprisonment? Know it to be essential to what is left of my reason? As air holes are essential to the insect captured in a bottle?

For after all, I've gained little knowledge of the practical world in which I might someday have had to survive. Literature could not have adorned my table or provided me with shelter from the storm. So I can read, yet stay safely dependent on you. And remain, of course, a freak.

But not a stupid one.

Because my intellect has glutted itself with the nourishment of the printed page, and from the vision of others I have formed an idea of justice. Thus, I can turn upon you now with the keen eye of the examiner. And in the dual role of victim and prosecutor, I will confront you with my charges.

You will protest, of course, that you do not understand.

In fact, you have often accused me of assaulting you with unfathomable words. Yet you must admit that my weapon pales before yours. For you have taught me, my father, that all the finely fashioned words in the world must yield to the ultimate means of articulation.

Must bow to brute force.

Mama, I'm bad. 'Cause I leave you alone. When I'm playing outside and it starts to rain and the trees get all shiny black and I can't see the sky. I see Broder coming with his lunch pail and his blue jacket on top of his head.

He says, Carlek, you goofy, come in now. But I make him kiss me first and he smells like wet grass and we go in, only it's dark in the kitchen so Broder turns on the light and makes me take my shoes off. But I don't smell any dinner and Broder says, Where's Mama? So I tell him you're asleep. Then he puts his lunch pail on the sink and I make my other shoe hurry off and I go after him. Your door's closed, and Broder looks at me and says, Mama— are you in there? And we wait and after awhile you say yes, only your voice sounds little, and we wait more and then we see the door opening. Broder says to me, Go get some juice now and I say, No, I want to see Mama, and we come in your room. It's kind of dark inside and your hair's all cloudy gold and you have on Daddy's undershirt and I see your plumpies underneath. You're walking away and you sit on your bed. You don't look at us and you don't say anything either. Broder holds me tight on my arm then and says, Go get some juice for Mama, and I like that so I say okay. I go in the kitchen and open up the icebox and get down the juice and I get your prettiest glass down, Mama, the one that looks like diamonds and won't break. I pour the juice real careful and it doesn't spill and I take one taste for me and then I bring it in. I see Broder sitting next to you and he tries to make me give him the juice and I say no. I go around him and hold up the juice for you, Mama. Only when you look at me your hand is on your face and I can see how funny your mouth looks and your eye is all closed and it's horrible all around your hand. It doesn't look like you, Mama, and I drop the juice. Broder gets real mad, and you put your arm around him and say, Don't, *min mus*. And the juice is running all over the yellow rug so Broder gets a towel and I say, I'll clean it, and he says, no, real meanlike. Then you say, Let Carlek do it, and you sound like you might cry and Broder says, I'll get some ice. I clean the juice up pretty good 'cause you only have to help me a little bit at the end. And after, I put the towel in the dirty clothes all by myself. Broder comes back with the funny gray ice thing and you put it over your eye and I see you make a face. Broder says, I hate him—I hate him more than the whole world. And you say, Not in front of Carlek. And then you stand up, Mama, and I see your leg and I don't like it 'cause it isn't all white now. It has big red places down it and on one part it is bleeding only the blood is dried up now. I know you got hurt. And Broder keeps on punching his other hand and he says, When did he come? And you look at me and you say, A little while ago. And then I know, Mama. I know you had a bad dream and the nightmonster came to hurt you. I went down for my nap and you were still pretty. But I got up real quiet and ate up all the crackers and went outside without asking and the nightmonster came. I left you alone, Mama. I was always bad.

I am very tired.

But the sun is up.

I have told you how much I love the sun.

It can bring out the loveliness in Almost Perfect Things, as it is doing now. I am sitting by the window and the morning sun is coming right into my hand. Nestled here is a tiny seashell. On the outside it is colored a modest charcoal gray, but its true beauty is inside—rainbow hues burnished with a lamina of pearl.

It came from Dean.

Let me begin at the beginning.

I had known Dean for only a few days last year when he asked if he could spend time with me on my sixteenth birthday. He still didn't know about my father's rules, and my first thought was: Impossible.

I had already deduced that when Dea.. learned the truth about my situation, I would probably lose him. So I made up a blatant falsehood about how sentimental my father can be about birthdays. In a moment of pure abandon, I also said I would try to slip away to the library for a little while on that special afternoon.

After hours of agonizing I devised a plan to tell my father I'd been asked to perform a puppet show at the library. And since it was within walking distance of our house, I wouldn't need a ride.

Despite all this creative planning, Jessie, the morning of my birthday was hellish. I saw again how easily my father can bring out the coward in me. He was up by eleven, but it was after one o'clock before I could bring myself to ask him about going. By that time he was sitting, comfortably disheveled and unwashed, in his favorite chair, trying to treat his Saturday night hangover with the "hair of the dog that bit him"—his Sunday morning Bloody Marys.

"I have a puppet show at the library at two," I finally began, saying each word carefully so they wouldn't tumble over each other.

He eased back into the recliner, his plaid robe gaping open at his chest, and kicked idly at the Sunday newspaper flung about him on the family room floor. "How long will you be?"

Trying to conceal my relief at this unexpected benevolence, I said, "Oh, about an hour for the show, the setup, and all, and about an hour to walk it." My pulse hammered as I thought: It's too late now, too late to turn back.

His face impassive, he peered down at the faintly pinkish ice cube in the bottom of his glass. "I could drive you then. That stage is heavy."

"It's okay, Dad. I don't need my stage today. The Children's Room already has one." Please no, I thought frantically. No snags. No risks.

"I'm the one who needs to walk." He pointed with friendly disdain at his expanding beer belly. "Maybe I should walk with you."

Suspicion, I wondered? A test? He'd never suggested walking anywhere with me before. I held myself steady, remembering that he often responds to reverse psychology. "That'd be good, Dad. It's only a mile and a half. You shouldn't get all that tired."

A slight crease appeared between his brows, and he proffered his empty glass for me to refill. "You sure don't need the exercise, baby. You're so damn thin."

I went to the kitchen and mixed his Bloody Mary, this time tucking a piece of celery into the glass. When I came back, he gave the drink a loving look. "That's my girl," he said. He drank deeply and licked his lips. "Perfect." He sighed. "Well, hell, it's your birthday. If you want to spend it with a bunch of little kids, I guess it's all right with me. Getting paid for this one?"

"No. I couldn't charge the library, Dad. Mrs. Lewis has been really nice to me. She really helped get the word out when we first moved here."

Dad nodded companionably. "Good public relations. That's smart."

"Anyway, I like doing a favor for the library," I said. "You know how much I use it."

He laughed. "I'll say so. Sometimes I'd think you'd rather be there than here with me. Especially lately. You've gone there practically everyday after school, haven't you?"

"It's this history project," I said, glancing at my watch. "The teacher is making demands as though we were college students." And I thought suddenly how easy it is for me to lie and how much I do it. It's almost as if every response I make to my father is calculated.

He patted his knee. "Come on over here and tell me good-bye."

I hesitated. "I'll be late, Dad."

"Late? Who do you think you are, girl? Lady Astor?" He set his drink down on the table beside him. "Come."

Afraid of losing the ground I'd won, I obeyed.

"Right here." He pointed to his lap.

I checked the windows automatically. In that house the family room faced the backyard and we weren't in anyone's direct line of vision. But habit prevailed.

He caught my hand and pulled me down onto his lap. "See? You're still small enough to sit here." The odor of booze enveloped us both now. "I don't care how old you are, you're still my little girl." He ruffled my hair with one hand. "My Goldilocks." Then he was frowning. "Only you don't have goldilocks anymore. Your hair is darker than it used to be, and you've cut it all off. Why don't you let your hair grow out, Carla?" He was whining now. "You know how I like your hair long." He put his finger under my chin and turned my face back to his. Then he smiled broadly, his teeth unbrushed, his breath unbearably foul, the stubble of his beard harsh against my cheek. "Say, you know that big dictionary you want? The Oxford one? Christ, that bugger's expensive. But if you let your hair grow out—and maybe put a little weight on—you just might be able to talk me into one."

He moved his legs as though seeking a more comfortable position, and I rose obligingly, relieved at any chance for separation. "Sit," he said, pulling me down again. "I'm not through talking to you." The congenial mood was starting to dissipate. "Well?"

"I'll try, Dad."

"Do it."

51

"Okay." Another lie, of course, since I knew I wouldn't.

Then he was plaintive again. "I need you, baby."

One of my father's favorite words—need. Such a little word, Jessie, to rule my life the way it does.

"I have to leave, Dad." I said it softly, ever so cautiously, but I knew my plans for the afternoon were disintegrating.

What kind of payment this time, Daddy? You Shylock of my freedom. What pound of flesh will you exact so I may earn a breath of precious air?

He stroked my leg slowly with his free hand, and at that moment, the affection in his touch was more repulsive to me than his lust.

Not now, Dad. No. Anytime but now.

Yet I could already feel myself shutting down that place inside me where love and longing do battle with hate. And I thought: What will it be today, Daddy? Will it be enough just to enjoy the pressure of your body against mine? Or will you require me to close the drapes, as you so often do, in order to desecrate the clean white wall with your filmed epics of human flesh?

Will today be all the more satisfying because you know it is my sixteenth birthday?

But a strange thing happened then. My father's rapid breathing began to subside, and when he spoke again, it was with an almost kindly gruffness. "Oh, go on, Carla. Do it. Get out of here."

Nearly undone by the swiftness of this change, I lifted myself off of his lap. His damp fingers trailed along my arm. "But be back no later than four."

I was trembling as I tucked my blouse into my jeans and moved quickly toward the doorway. "I won't be late, Dad. I promise."

And it appeared that he was letting me go, Jessie. Yes,

he was. As a real father might do. A regular normal everyday Dad.

"It looks cold out," he called after me. "Take a sweater."

More fatherly still. What has possessed him? I wondered, feeling slightly faint now. I'd left my denim jacket and the backpack containing my puppets optimistically in the front hall. I opened the door, my last picture of him still imprinted on my brain. Sitting there in his plaid robe and the worn-out slippers he won't part with for anything. My father, looking oddly weak and vulnerable and so very alone.

And even here, in the clean October sunshine, I could feel it, Jessie—the guilt. Over this new brand of deception. For I was lying this time not out of concern for his feelings, nor as an unavoidable measure for my own self-defense, but for my own pleasure, the consummate pleasure of being in the presence of my friend.

You will laugh at me perhaps, but an even deeper guilt was there, too. Because I felt I had deserted my father. The hideous part of him now seemed only a memory, and in its place was a helpless and abandoned child.

Yet the lure of my emancipation was too strong. And guilt fell away as I walked in the aching sweetness of this freedom. Along the quiet streets as the Sunday people worked on their lawns and gardens, I breathed in the scent of fresh-cut grass and listened to the sound of a basketball driving against a backboard. I moved along the streets absorbing everything around me.

And I thought: I am free, and like a treasure stored deep within me is the knowledge that in a few minutes I will be with Dean.

I closed my eyes and imagined him reaching out to me along the languorous streets—his voice dreamlike in the lyrical cadences of the Song of Songs:

Arise my love
My dove
My beautiful one
And come.

He was waiting in the periodical section of the library, other Sunday readers sitting peacefully nearby. Behind them a bay window framed the afternoon sky and a generous sweep of lawn. The day was painted in the most vibrant colors I had ever seen.

I stood back for a moment to watch him waiting there, a newspaper unopened in his lap, his glossy hair brushed carefully and that dapper look about him that sets Dean apart from everyone else.

I saw him turn to look at the clock on the wall, then open his paper. I was two minutes early, and a little jittery, so I allowed myself that time for observation.

You must admit that it offends one's sense of order. How strange the two of us look together, I mean—Dean, with a face right out of a Beautiful Baby contest, and Carla, his tomboy sidekick—surely the ultimate shatterers of the masculine/feminine ideal.

Or do I flatter myself? Perhaps I am more of a nonentity, too plain to be perceived at all. Colorless, odorless and tasteless—like the perfect poison.

At exactly two o'clock I moved toward Dean, wondering why I hadn't given at least a thought to what I was wearing. Wishing I didn't look the way I did.

But when Dean saw me, he smiled. And that smile was a blending of eagerness and affection that seemed to erase all the doubts I had ever experienced.

"You made it!" he called out. Several people looked up at us, and suddenly I was proud. Because it was me bringing that radiance into his dark eyes.

"Where can we go?" he asked, still smiling, not hiding his feelings the way most guys do.

"The Community Room," I told him. "Mrs. Burnett says I can use it to practice—when it's empty."

And it was. I switched on the light, and we settled ourselves in a corner, away from the door so we could hear someone come in before they would see us.

"You really know your way around here," Dean said. He nodded at my backpack. "Did you bring me something?"

"Only my puppets."

He looked even more delighted. "Great. You can give me my own private show."

I could feel myself blushing. "Oh, no, that's not why I brought them."

"Why did you then?"

"Well, I told my father I was coming here to do a play."

Dean looked startled. "You lied to him?"

"Just—I didn't want to hurt his feelings. You know, because it's my birthday and all."

He looked away from me. "I hate lies."

And I wanted to say, Truth is a luxury, Dean. A privilege.

"Doesn't he understand? I mean—you wanting to be with somebody else, too?"

I don't know why I did it just then, but at that moment I glanced at my watch. Dean reached over and took hold of my wrist to do the same. Instinctively, I flinched.

"Hey." He looked wounded. "I just wanted to see, too. You can't stay long, can you?"

I was tense with embarrassment. "Till three-thirty. I'm sorry. When someone comes toward me like that . . ."

His face held the suggestion of a pout.

"You don't understand. It isn't you, Dean. Really. I just wasn't expecting it right then."

"Okay. I'm not trying to be a pain or anything. But I sure don't want to repulse anybody."

It's funny. It hadn't yet occurred to me that Dean could be insecure. I guess I've always thought self-doubt was my exclusive domain. "You aren't repulsive to me. I'm just nervous, I guess."

He grinned unexpectedly. "Me, too."

"I was hoping you'd tell me about you. Your life and all."

"Have you got five hours? Or ten? I have a very—uh—interesting life. If you're into soap operas. Like Lynette, my foster mother—she loves to hear about my life."

Just take control of this, I told him silently, because I don't know what to do.

"Well—what then?" He hesitated. "Where should I start?"

"Your birth?"

He looked amused. "Okay. That's easy. I can give it to you straight out of my case record. I sneaked a look at it when my caseworker had to leave her office once. Those people have a real knack for putting everything that's ever happened to you in a paragraph. Mr. Freed—he's my journalism teacher—would be really impressed." He paused. "So anyway—Baby Boy Burroughs was born on July 19th——"

"Baby who? You're going too fast for me."

"Okay. 'Baby Boy' because I wasn't given a first name for a while."

"How come?"

"Now let me tell this my way, Carla. It's confusing as heck, so just try and stay with me. I wasn't officially named because my mother was having this big fight with the hospital over my last name, which she wanted to be

Lowrey, after my father. Since they weren't married then, the hospital wanted me to be Burroughs, which was her last name. Or not so much the hospital, I guess, but the adoption agency—because she was seriously considering giving me away and all. And I didn't get a first name right off because she figured the adopting parents would name me. She was also very heavily into postpartum depression and not feeling too creative. Or so the story goes."

"I see." But I didn't really grasp it all, and I was amazed by the detached way Dean was speaking, as though he didn't care.

He leaned back on the wooden bench where we sat and stretched his arms high above his head. "See how long this is taking? And we haven't even got past the first week of my life."

I shook my head. I wasn't bored at all. But it hurt to see the coldness in his eyes.

"So anyway, my mother ended up keeping me after all because she and my father decided to get married. And then she named me Dean. It's after that actor from the fifties—the one who died—James Dean." Looking tired all of a sudden, he gave me a lopsided smile. "She had a picture of him in my room for years. A scene from that movie he made, *Rebel Without a Cause*. Isn't that weird? It's a wonder she didn't light a candle to him every night."

I didn't like the way he was talking about her, Jessie. His bitterness. I was even beginning to feel angry.

"So when the little family got together, sometime before I was a year old, all went well for at least a month. Or so I hear. I'm not too sure because I can't ever get anything firsthand from my mother. And I was into teething rings and rubber duckies at the time."

My tension eased a little when he said that. "I know what you mean."

"You do?"

"Well, about wanting to know things."

He pursed his lips. "Yeah—and they won't tell you."

"Right."

"Anyway, it turned out that one measly little woman just wasn't enough for my dad—or even two or three actually. I guess he was trying to get my mother to divorce him. Like trying to break a lease. After one big night out, he actually brought one of his girl friends home, with my mom there and all. Wow." He looked at me directly now. "God—do you believe anybody could take that much sh-h . . . uh, aggravation?"

And I thought, Yes, I do. Even though I knew he wouldn't understand.

"Why are you looking at me that way, Carla?"

"Well, it must have been pretty hard for her. Maybe she didn't have enough money to be on her own."

"Huh?" He began toying uneasily with the tag on my backpack. "Yeah. That's true I guess. I mean, I can remember later. The way she struggled to support us. After she left Mason Hinkle. Her second husband. And—Jim Yaeger. Her third." He was looking right at me now, waiting for my reaction.

"I'm sorry," I said.

His eyes darkened with pain. "I'm getting ahead of myself, aren't I? I mean, Mason Hinkle deserves at least a word or two. I was starting school about then. And where my father was a louse and a bastard, Mason Hinkle was a weirdo. He was super eccentric. He liked to read a lot, and he had this thing for saving newspapers. At home he had a whole newspaper room. Papers and magazines piled up almost to the ceiling. You couldn't even see where the windows were anymore."

"But why?" I asked. "Everything's in the library. On microfilm."

"I know. And I'm sure he did, too. But the guy was wacko. He'd always say, 'I'm gonna read that article on such-and-such this week, so don't throw it away.' Only he said that about all the articles—all eleven thousand and eighty of them. It got to where moths and stuff would fly out of these papers. The place was a health hazard. Mom divorced him when I was ten. By then she'd finished nursing school, which helped a lot." Dean stood up for a moment, then sat down again. He seemed as wound up now as my father sometimes gets. "It was at one of the hospitals where she met Jim Yaeger—he was a nurse, too. They were together for about three years." He drew in his breath. "It was good for me. For the first time in my life." He fell silent for a moment. Then he said, "God, Carla. I sure am being an ass. I've got to be boring the heck out of you by now."

"No," I said softly, and found myself wanting to hold him.

His mouth tightened a little. "I've told you so much already. Let's let it rest now."

"Sure," I said. In a strange way I, too, was relieved that he stopped. But in another way I was sorry.

"It's your turn now," he said brightly. "Now I get to hear about you."

"Dean, could we just not talk? For a minute? Just kind of sit here like this?"

He took my hand in his and the movement seemed natural. "Okay. For a minute." And it was the kind of silence I dream about having with you, Jessie. We were just together like that, the two of us, and for the first time in years I was no longer feeling alone.

Finally he said, "If we do this much more, I might end up crying or something. And really embarrass you."

I squeezed his hand. "It's okay. I wouldn't mind."

"No. Enough stalling. Tell me about you now."

I looked at my watch again.

"Plenty of time," he said.

"Well—okay. There's just my dad and me."

"Right."

"And we've moved a lot." I shrugged my shoulders. "There's nothing more to tell."

"What happened to your mom?"

"She died when I was born."

He moved closer to me. "You're so tense, Carla. You really hate this, don't you?"

I nodded. "I'm shy I guess."

He motioned to my backpack. "Maybe I could talk to those guys instead."

I was stunned. Because it was as though he knew even then. About my Voices. "Oh, no."

"Then just tell me about them. Each one. Especially Punkey."

And I warned myself: Danger, Carla. And I said, "I don't know. . ."

His expression changed. "I get it. I'm supposed to open up to you, right? Spill my guts all over the place. But you get to stay inside your shell."

I opened the backpack. "You can look at them," I said. I took Punkey out first and gave him to Dean. It was strange then, even magical. As though I were giving him something alive. And it was beautiful to watch the way Dean handled him. He held my monkey in his arms like a baby.

"Tell me about him, Carla."

But words wouldn't come, not from me. I couldn't speak for Punkey now because he was ready to speak for himself.

"I don't know," I said. "I can't."

Dean gave Punkey a helpless look. "So how 'bout that, little guy?"

Then I was reaching for Punkey and settling him into position on my hand. "How 'bout what?" Punkey said, sassylike.

Dean smiled. "Well, hi there! It's good to see you again."

"So what's happening, Dean?"

"Just a lazy Sunday. What's with you?"

"I've got love problems. With Kristal. She's starting to like Mymouse more than she likes me. Even though I'm *much* better looking."

Dean hesitated. "Maybe it's your personality."

"My what? Look, you! I have more charm than any other monkey in the world. And the day I can't compete with him—shit!"

Dean's eyes lit up as eagerly as those of some of the babies I've played to. "First off, Punkey, there's your language."

"My what?"

"The way you talk. Have you ever thought about cleaning it up? People don't like that."

Punkey nearly bounced right off my hand. "Tough taco! And besides, Kristal isn't a people. She's a parrot. I know what the problem is anyway. It's all his fault—Lord Punchkiss. He fucks up everything."

"Okay, little guy. That's just what I mean. You can't go around using a word like that."

"Oh, yeah? Says who?"

"Me. I would definitely think twice about it."

"Think twice? I usually don't even think once about things. Thinking is for the birds."

Dean's brown eyes shone. "Like Kristal? Then maybe I'd better hear her side of the story."

"Now that's a dumb idea," said Punkey. "When you hear two sides of a story, all you get is confused."

"Now come on, Punkey. Be fair."

"Fair! When I see those beady little eyes and that darling beak and those shiny red tailfeathers, I don't care about fair."

"Well, you should," Dean said.

"Not now, Broder. I have a feeling it wouldn't be fun. And besides, I'm getting tired."

"Broder? Is that what you called me?"

"Yeah. I'm going now. So long."

Punkey wanted his nap, so I put him into the backpack.

"Why did he call me that?" Dean asked.

"He made a mistake," I said casually. "Punkey has this thing about names. And he especially doesn't like his own."

"Why not?"

"He thinks it reminds people of Punchkiss. And that really bothers him." I was speaking freely then, Jessie, just as if that were a safe thing to do.

"Broder," he mused. "I wonder where he got that."

And then it hit, Jessie—sudden faintness, and a tremor through my body.

Dean was concentrating. "It reminds me of something." He cocked his head to one side. "Oh, yeah—*bruder*. It reminds me of the word *bruder*."

I could feel the icy sweat in my hand.

"It's German," he went on. "I learned it from Jim—my step-dad. He used to teach me a new word every day." His eyes were misty now. "Oh, right—that's it. It means brother."

He turned to me. Gave me a kindly, searching look, then drew me close.

I clung to him. And for a moment I could almost believe we were together again, Broder and I, in our sled, flying down and deeper down the snowy hill.

"Carla?"

I opened my eyes and moved back from him a little. I pulled my backpack toward me. "I have to go."

His look of disappointment touched me.

When we got outside he reached into his pocket, looking suddenly as shy as a child, and brought out a piece of paper that had been folded over several times. Along with a tiny seashell.

"I know I haven't said happy birthday yet, Carla. But it's in here. I mean, you can read this when you get home." I slipped the paper into the back pocket of my jeans, could feel it there glowing like a jewel.

Then he said, "This isn't anything." He put the seashell into my hands before I could look at it and closed my fingers around it. "But it is. At least it means a lot to me. I found it at the beach once when I was with Jim. He spent the whole day with me, and it was super important to me. I've kept this around to remember it by."

My throat constricted painfully because I knew I wasn't worthy. "Are you sure?"

"Yeah. I want you to have it. I could have bought you something—no I couldn't, 'cause I'm flat broke right now—but this is different. Special. To me anyway." He looked self-conscious. "Not that it's worth anything. . . ."

"Yes it is," I said. Then I took his hand and brought it to my lips. And the thank you inside me was so large I couldn't begin to say it. We both just stood there looking at each other for a while and when it was time to go he walked me part of the way home and I knew the whole time it wasn't just my sixteenth birthday anymore.

It had become the best day of my life.

That seashell, Jessie. The one Dean gave me a year ago today?

Do you understand how precious one seashell can be?

It is here in my hand.

And I am still remembering.

When I arrived home from the library that afternoon, my father had scrawled "out showing property" on the kitchen blackboard, and I realized his office must have called him in. I cleaned up the glasses and broken peanut shells in the family room and pictured my father casting off his Sunday lethargy to greet the world outside as though he'd never heard of a hangover. He has that talent.

His absence was an extension of the miracle that day had become. Without fear of being disturbed, I would be able to enjoy my gift from Dean and read what he'd written to me.

In my room I pulled Dean's note out of my back pocket and sat down in my rocking chair. The piece of paper had been folded until it was almost as small as the seashell itself.

You'll laugh at me, Jessie, but I was afraid to open it. The unexpected—a surprise of any kind—always fills me with an odd kind of dread.

But I had to know. The paper opened to the size of a letter, and as soon as I saw the "Dear Carla" in Dean's small, mostly printed handwriting, my fears began to subside.

For a birthday present, I know a seashell isn't much. But this one is part me of because I use it to remember a special day. It happened when I was twelve and my Mom was married to this guy named Jim Yaeger, who was the best father I've had along the way.

One day Jim took me and my dog Dusty to the beach at Corona del Mar and we brought a picnic lunch that Jim and I made ourselves. I'd never done that before, usually just bought hot dogs at a stand. When we were too tired to swim anymore we built a sandcastle that Dusty kept messing up. We talked a lot that day and then Jim asked me if he could adopt me. I guess that made the whole thing just about perfect, and I said yes.

Well, this story doesn't have such a happy ending because my real father, Ray Lowrey, said I was his son and he wasn't going to sign any papers. Only he was living in Tennessee and I hadn't seen him for years. My Mom said he probably didn't want to let me go just because somebody else wanted me and she was going to go for all the back child support he owed no matter how much it cost in legal fees. So my real father thought it over for a couple of months and then he said it would be okay for Jim to adopt me. Only by that time my Mom and Jim were getting a divorce.

The main point is that the day at the beach was the closest time I've ever had with another human being and I'll never forget what Jim tried to do. I still see him once in a while. He got married to this really sweet woman named Melanie two years ago and they have a baby now.

Anyway, I guess the seashell is about caring, which is why I decided to give it to you. I think you're about as lonely inside as I was then and maybe this little seashell will help sometimes.

So, happy birthday, Carla, and hang in there!
    Love,
    Dean

Of all his letters, Jessie, this is the one I still read over and over again. Because he hardly knew me at all then, and yet he trusted me with something he cherished more than anything else he had.

Now you can see, can't you? You can see why I love him.

Mama, I'm real quiet now and I don't scream only it's too late. When it was dark he came in and said Be still, and then he hurt me with his finger, but I made noise and Broder woke up and jumped on my bed and tried to fight. Only the nightmonster got a big mad face and he squeezed Broder on the neck and threw him down and Broder got all quiet. And the nightmonster went away.

Please, Mama, come help us.
You have to come now.

Mymouse: How long will we wait?
Kristal: It's too late. It's our fate.
Leona Ly: Hush, sweet babies—I'm here.

It's Sunday morning.

I watched from my window as the people who live next door came home from church today. A beautiful family with a father and mother, and two little girls wearing dresses and tiny white shoes. The younger child, whose wavy hair always gleams like polished copper, tried to do a handstand on the front lawn and ignominiously dirtied her clothes. When her father scolded her, I heard him call her Sara.

A little while later I found myself standing at the window of our guest bedroom upstairs, watching Sara swim in her backyard pool. And I watched her mother who was stretched out nearby like a big sleek cat in the sun.

I am thinking of Sara now.

I wonder if she would like my Upside Down Theatre.

I pray that she is safe.

While my father was at his workbench in the garage this afternoon, I painted the small bathroom off our front hall. Not much of a job really, but even after a steaming shower, my muscles still ache.

It's starting again. The long silent hours of work we will put in on this house in our quest for perfection.

Who was it who said that everything changes, yet everything stays the same?

I'm alone now. And thinking about the tightrope my life has always been lived on.

Last year he imperiled that equilibrium.

My loving friend. Dean.

Soon after our meeting at the library he asked me to go to a movie with him. And I knew the time had come to disclose the rules that straitjacket Carla Jean Hughes.

I remember so well how it happened, the two of us walking from school to the library that day.

Dean was excited. "I don't have to babysit for the twins tomorrow night, and I earned some money yesterday. So we can see any movie you want."

"I don't go to movies," I said.

"Why not?"

"I'm not allowed. Not on dates, I mean."

He stopped in front of a small grocery store and just stared at me. "Your father?"

"He's pretty strict."

Dean looked incredulous. "You mean you *never* go out? At all?"

I nodded.

"Carla, that's nuts." He began to rub his forehead as though he had a headache. "Hey, be honest with me. Is this for real?"

And I was growing more embarrassed by the second. "Yes," I said.

"Wow, and I thought Mr. Sloane was tough. I can't believe this. I always think it's just foster kids who have it bad."

"It isn't all bad," I said defensively.

"Oh, sure it isn't. Not at all. Just this guy trying to possess you or something."

Fear and exasperation flared in me. "Dean, don't analyze him."

His smile was sardonic. "I have a feeling my shrink would love to meet your father."

I froze.

"Come on, Carla. Don't look like that."

I could feel my heartbeat beginning to slow again. "Don't talk about him. Please. It isn't fair."

"But I never see you with girl friends either. Do you have any social life at all?"

"If I don't, it's my fault. I'm shy. Really shy."

"But no wonder. I mean, you're in jail, you know? Carla you ought to see somebody. You need to get help."

I didn't like it, Jessie—not one thing about the way that conversation was going.

"Well, I'd like to meet him," Dean said. "Show him what a nice guy I am."

My heart seemed to stop again. "Can't we just keep on the way we are? I mean, seeing each other at school every day?"

Dean started walking again and I followed. I could tell from his movements that he was angry now.

"I can't help it, Dean. I have to do what he says. He's my father."

He was walking even faster now, making it hard for me to keep up.

"I'm sorry," I said earnestly. "I'm really sorry."

He stopped dead in his tracks and turned to me. "Hey—that's why you wouldn't let me walk you all the way home last Sunday. Isn't it? And why you lied to him—about meeting me at the library?"

I felt ashamed.

"In a way, you were lying to me, too," he went on. "That's what people do, you know? They lie. A lot."

I couldn't look at him.

"This just doesn't make any sense at all. That you won't even let me talk to him. He's got to let you go out sometime. Only I don't think you really want him to." He shrugged. "I don't mean anything to you at all."

Pain swelled in my stomach and settled there like a rock. "You do, Dean. I love seeing you. It's—it's everything."

"Then I don't get it. I mean, I've been feeling that way, too. You've been the best thing about this crummy school."

"I just can't help it," I said.

His eyes narrowed. "So. You're going to stay this way forever."

"I—I don't know."

"Well, I don't know either." He began walking again, as fast as before. "But I can't handle it, okay?"

We were rounding the last corner and the library was in sight.

"Even now what we're doing is like sneaking. By his rules anyway," Dean said bitterly. "I won't let anybody hide me away like that. It's only going to make me start feeling bad about myself again."

He stopped in front of the library. A fine mist of rain was beginning to fall, but Dean didn't seem to notice. "I guess we shouldn't even be out here, right?" His voice was heavy with sarcasm. "Who knows if he might drive by and see us?"

There was more justice than he knew in that accusation.

"So let me know," he said. "Just let me know if you ever stop being some kind of prisoner."

And after that, Jessie, he wouldn't talk to me. Wouldn't see me.

It was a quality of isolation I had never experienced before. It lasted for seven agonizing days.

Then it ended. And with a joke. The kind Dean most enjoys—a dramatic one.

It happened on the following Wednesday night with the sound of pebbles hitting my bedroom window. I still don't know how Dean found out where we lived, let alone how he knew which room belonged to me.

When I opened the window he was standing right outside in the moonlight, and I could see his hands clasped together like Romeo's, only he was saying, "Rapunzel, Rapunzel, let down your hair."

By some miracle my father wasn't at home, nor did he return until long after Dean was gone. And of course Dean never understood why I was so afraid while he was there, why I kept urging him to leave.

Like my father, Dean doesn't give up easily. And all last year he kept probing into my life with questions I can't answer. Alluding to what he calls my outrageous situation, even daring to call my father a liar and me a fool.

But who is *he* to be giving *me* ultimatums? At least I live in my own home with my real father. Instead of bouncing like a ball from one foster family to the next.

Oh, God, Jessie—how cruel that was. How unfeeling. Especially from me, when I'm just luckier than he is.

It isn't Dean's fault he's in a foster home anyway. And the Sloanes really did care for him. They even invited him to move to Oregon with them last summer. Dean just didn't want to go that far away.

He even said he didn't want to be that far from me.

Then his caseworker said he was getting too "independent" to live in another family. So they moved him into a group home supposedly for boys "like himself." Which is absurd, of course. Since there is no one else in the world like Dean Lowrey. Let alone a whole group of them living somewhere in the Wilshire district of Los Angeles.

Oh, Dean. It was so wonderful last year on my birthday. With you.

At midnight tonight I will be seventeen.

I wonder where you are now. And if it's possible that you remember.

No.
I am alone.

Mama, it's my birthday and we're standing on the boardwalk. You're turned sideways and bending down to look in your purse and your hair is around your head in a braid all smooth and shining white in the sun. You get out some coins and hold them in your hand and they are winking at me. You smile and say, There is just enough for you and Broder to ride the Cyclone Racer. I'm glad 'cause I have to wait till today, till I'm six, to go on it. You give Broder the money and then you say to me, There's only enough to go once, Carlek, but when we get home I have a big surprise for you. I say, Oh, Mama, I think I'm too scared to ride and you laugh and Broder takes my hand and we go.

The ride is made of old wood and the paint is coming off in long white peels. The man in the funny green hat takes our tickets and lets Broder and me get in the car and it's warm in there and we start to move. At first we move up real slow and I look back to find you, Mama. You're all alone down there and you're getting littler and I'm scared of that, but you are waving. And pretty soon we get clear to the top and Broder holds me tight and my heart is kicking inside me and I hide my eyes and we start to fall and I scream at Broder and he's laughing and everybody screams. The breath jumps out of me and then we make it down smooth and we start climbing back up again and I can't see you anymore but the ocean is all sparkles and we are almost at the top and we get slow and then I hide my eyes and Broder yells out my name and we fly down again down and deeper down. . . .

Before we get on the bus to go home, you make us put on our sweaters and on the way Broder teases me about my present and what do I think he got me and he tickles me under my arm so I tickle his neck. I nearly trip getting off the bus, Mama, and you lift me up and hold me for a minute. We climb up the steps and go inside and then you say to us, Go in the bedroom now while I fix up something. So we go in our room and Broder says, You won't ever guess your surprise, and then we hear somebody at the front door. It's Daddy and he's smiling with a big nice face and he says he has a special surprise for me. Then you bring in a white cake, Mama, with six red candles on it and everybody sings and you give me a necklace made of little gold beads and Broder gives me his own dump truck that he loves and I love, too, and Daddy says I get to go on a trip with him. So later you give me a sack with clothes in it, Mama, and you hold me extra tight and whisper in my ear, Don't be scared, and I say, Mama, you come, too, and you don't let go of me and you say, It's all right, Carlek, it's only till tomorrow. Then Broder hugs me and says he wants to come only Daddy says no and you say to Broder, No, my mouse, you stay with me. And then Daddy and me go. Daddy goes first down the steps 'cause it's dark, and when we're driving, he says, Are you big enough to go on a trip with me? And I say yes, 'cause I love to go on trips and anyway we're already on the trip. And he says, Aren't you scared without Mama? And I say no, and I get out the piece of birthday cake she gave me and I feed Daddy some right while he's driving and he laughs and I laugh, too. And it's so good to be with my Daddy 'cause I didn't see him for a long time and I giggle and he lets me eat more cake 'cause he says we won't stop to eat for a long, long time. It gets later and the sky is so pretty and the trees are all on fire and the lawns are sprinkled all over with gold. We drink chocolate out of Broder's Thermos and I say, Broder wants his Thermos, and Daddy looks at me and says, Oh, he does, does he?

And then we laugh 'cause Broder doesn't need his Thermos till Monday. But I get tired after a while and later my tummy starts to feel bad and I say, I'm sick, Daddy, and he says, Well, we can't stop now. Try to go to sleep. So I do and I lay my head on his leg and he pats my hair and I don't care if his pants are scratchy 'cause I get to have my head there and I feel safe.

When I wake up it's all black in the car except where the little lights are that tell Daddy how to drive and I feel better only I'm so hungry and I tell Daddy and he says we have to wait. There's no more birthday cake to eat and we go a long way and then I say, Are we almost there? And Daddy says, We have a long way more yet, but you'll like this trip. And after he doesn't say anything for a while, Daddy says, I have something to tell you and I want you to listen real good to me. I want you to be like a big person, okay? And I say I can 'cause I'm big now and I go to school just like Broder. And Daddy says, You and me are going to be gone for a long time. We're moving far away. And I ask him, When will Mama come? And he pats me on the knee a little bit and he says, Now that's just it. That lady you call Mama—she isn't really your mama. She's a lady I paid to take care of you. A babysitter. Because I couldn't keep you with me before. I don't understand him and I say it. So Daddy says, That lady is not your mother. She just took care of you for a while. And I say, She's my mama, so he'll know. No, no, he says, when you were born, your mama died and went to heaven. You don't even remember who she is. And I say, My mama? I can feel the tears squeezing up in my eyes. My mama didn't die though, I say. He is getting mad at me now because he is hurting my leg with his hand. No, not this one, he says. She isn't your real mama. She was just taking care of you. And then I feel like I have to go pinka and I tell him and he says, Not now. We're miles from a bathroom now. You'll have to hold it. And I say okay because I'm scared, and then he says, You and me will be together from now on. We'll be living in a big city. What about Broder? I ask him, and Daddy says, Broder is her son and he can't come with us because he isn't your real brother. You're his daddy, I say, only then I feel a worse squeeze on my leg. No, I'm not, Daddy says real loud. I want my mama, I say, and the tears are coming out now and my tummy is scared again. Don't be a crybaby, he says, 'cause I hate crybabies worse than anything. I'm sorry, I say, and I stop crying fast and the hurt on my leg gets lighter. Only now I have to go pinka real bad. I know I'm going to wet my pants, Daddy. Please can I go? I can't hold it anymore. And he says, Okay, you slide up next to me and I'll hold it for you. And I sit close to him, and he puts his hand over it and presses on me. Oh, no, Daddy, I cry to him. It makes me go. I wet my pants. Then he gets real mad and he says, Shame on you, and he makes the car go slow and then he stops the car and I get more scared. My pants are all wet and I hold the rest of the pinka in me but I still need to go some more. And then he looks at me in a funny way and he says, See what you did? See? You didn't hold it in like I told you to. You got the car seat all wet. And I try not to cry and I say, I'm sorry, and I hold my legs together real tight so no more will come out.

You're bad, he says to me. It's pretty dark, but I can see his big mad face. You're all dirty now and you've got piss in your pants and all over the seat. Now we have to clean all that up. And then more is coming out of me 'cause I can't hold it anymore and I'm so scared and I don't want him to see only he does and his mouth opens up and his face gets ugly and he screams at me, Stop it! Then he slaps me real hard and the sparkle things come in my eyes and he pushes me down on the seat and says, You can clean it up yourself then. That'll be the way. Lick it clean. I say, No, please don't make me, Daddy. I can't lick it. It's pinka. And he laughs and says, What did you call it? Does *she* say that? Well, it's piss and you can lick it up. You can do anything I tell you to do. Right now! And he holds my face down on the seat and I close my eyes real tight and the pinka tastes sharp and he pushes my head around till I lick it all up. And he is laughing. Then I am done and I feel all chokey and he starts up the car and he says to me, You liked that, didn't you? And I say, Can I put my panties on now? And he shakes his head and says, You didn't answer me yet. What, Daddy? I asked you whether you liked that piss, he says. Oh, no, I say, and I start to cry. And he says, Yes, you do, crybaby. You like it. Say you like it. No, Daddy, I can't help it. Daddy gets mad again, and he says, Is that how she taught you? To say no to your daddy? Then he puts his hand on my leg again and squeezes. Say you liked it. You have to. And then I see what it is, so I say I liked it and then he lets go my leg and it hurts bad and I don't think of anything else for a long time.

After a while Daddy says, I don't want you to be afraid of anybody in the whole world except me. I don't say anything back to him. And he says, 'cause I'm big. And I say, Great big. And he says, We're going to be together always. You just mind me and I'll be good to you. Understand? I say, Yes, Daddy. Then he gives me a kiss, soft like the way you do, Mama.

Where are you, Mama?

I wait for you forever, only you don't come.

I tried not to write to you tonight, Jessie. I even tried to forget you.

It seems I need you too much.

I am still thinking about birthdays.

And I'm thinking of the woman I called Mama all those years ago.

I can almost see her face. A fairy queen with eyes the color of honey and white-gold hair. I remember her, even though there is no time I can remember well before I began to live alone with my father. What happened during those first five years remains dreamlike, unfixed in my mind. Except that now and then a moment will come to me out of that early darkness like a firefly, only to vanish before I can hold it in my hands. In that moment I can smell the warm fragrances of a kitchen or hear a soft scrap of foreign-sounding words.

Sometimes I can even feel her arms around me.

Yes. Shadowy as they are, recollections of this other life sometimes cling to me. Like my memory of a boy, a boy who wouldn't let anyone hurt me. Who let me fly his kite and ride his sled with him and call him Broder.

Until I knew better, I believed them to be my mother and brother. But Dad says they were only people I stayed with for a while, people who took care of me while he was traveling on his job—Mrs. Andrews and her son Broderick.

And they both disappeared from my life on the day I turned five.

So you see, Jessie, birthdays can bring sadness to some of us. And separation.

They can even bring death.

Like the death of my real mother—Jean Mallory Hughes.

While she was giving birth to me, my mother's leg became poisoned. And after just a few days, it was over.

So now you will understand.

Everything would have been all right if I hadn't killed her.

* * *

I'm so confused.

I dozed off for a while and awakened to the smell of blood. It came from cuts on my body, half-healed cuts that were opened up again.

Only I don't remember that part at all.

I cleaned myself up, but the spots on my quilt won't come out.

It doesn't matter. This quilt is mine. It's all mine.

And it keeps me warm.

It's nearly midnight now. I am lying warm under my quilt and my Voices speak into the darkness around me.

Mymouse: It's easy to see why I love you, Leona Ly.

Leona Ly: Dear Mymouse.

Mymouse: Because you have soulful eyes. And if I look long enough, I could fall right into them.

Leona Ly: Don't do that, though.

Mymouse: I won't. But would it be all right if I become a child now?

Leona Ly: Yes, Mymouse. Only you'll have to be—an old child.

Mymouse: I see. It's because I know too much, isn't it?

Leona Ly: I'm afraid so.

Mymouse: Oh, Leona Ly, how can I learn less? How can I grow down instead of up?

Leona Ly: There *is* a way, Mymouse. You can do it by remembering Almost Perfect Things.

Mymouse: What? But what are they?

Leona Ly: Almost Perfect Things are—well, when the wind touches a tree branch full of snow.

Mymouse: You mean, the way it looks? When the snow comes twinkling down like diamonds?

Leona Ly: That's it! And the way sunlight comes gleaming through icicles—

Mymouse: —and when the trees are all on fire.

Leona Ly:	That's it exactly, Mymouse. Keep remembering those things and you'll get small again.
Mymouse:	Thank goodness, Leona Ly. 'Cause I'm too young to be this old.
Leona Ly:	Oh, I agree.
Mymouse:	And then will you be my mother? The way you are with Punkey and Kristal?
Leona Ly:	Yes!
Mymouse:	And you won't be impatient with me? You'll always be kind and tender?
Leona Ly:	Sometimes I might get angry, Mymouse. But I'll never hurt you.
Mymouse:	Never?
Leona Ly:	Never.
Mymouse:	(Snuggling up to her) I can see it, Leona Ly.
Leona Ly:	What can you see?
Mymouse:	Your soul. I can see it in your eyes.

It's over, Jessie.

The digital clock on my desk is bleeping green numbers at me: 4:29A.M.

And what happened tonight when he came home—I think it might have been my fault. Yes. I do think it was.

When you live with a man like my father, you learn many things. You learn about what you can say, which questions you can ask, and when you can ask them.

But tonight I was stirred by an impatience even I don't understand. It's this new insanity, Jessie. The pieces of me don't want to hold together anymore.

And I pushed him too hard.

Sometime after midnight he came home and woke me up, wanting to talk and asking me to make him some coffee. I smelled liquor on him, but he seemed in a mild, even pensive mood, and I was sure he wasn't drunk.

While we waited for the coffee to brew, he sat at the

kitchen table and told me he'd closed a big sale at the beach tonight. Only instead of elation, a kind of bewilderment shone in his eyes. "Things are better for me every day, Carly."

Later, as he drank his coffee, an unusual silence fell between us. I found myself drawn in by this benevolent variation in his mood.

Our silence made me bold. "I've been thinking all day, Dad. About her."

He looked at me thoughtfully. "What?"

"My mother, I mean."

He sighed a deep, long-suffering sigh. "Do you have any idea how fucking often you bring this up?"

"I'm sorry."

"Jesus, girl. Let the dead rest."

"I know. I just miss having a mother."

His blue eyes grew hard. "What the hell! Do you think *I* had a mother?"

Since I already knew how he felt about his mother, I didn't reply.

"What a miserable rabbit that woman was. Never opened her mouth when he was around and didn't have a hell of a lot to say when he wasn't. Wouldn't stand up for any of *us* either. Just sniffled and whined over every goddamned little thing."

"Was she scared of him?"

"Yeah, I suppose. He was the one in charge anyway." My father was turning the thick white coffee mug around and around in his hands. "He figured we'd have to be tough to make it in this world. And that's the one thing the old bastard was right about." He gave me a sly smile. "You know, I came *that* close to picking up the phone tonight and calling him. I felt like letting the son of a bitch know all this good stuff that's happening to me." He paused. "Think I should?"

I was startled at being consulted on this question. "Sure, Dad."

The lines between his brows deepened. "Maybe so. Maybe so. There's nothing he can do to me now, right? And I wouldn't tell him where we are or anything. Just give him a few pertinent facts about how well we've done for ourselves."

I decided to try and divert my father from this well-worn path. "Did he know my mother?"

"Who?"

"My grandfather."

He pulled at his ear. His eyes were wary. "Oh, yeah, sure. Not well or anything. And he didn't like her, of course."

My pulse quickened. Periodically my father will reveal something new like this. "Why not, Dad?"

For a moment guilt showed in his eyes. "Who knows? He didn't need reasons for things. I told you the whole goddamned family is screwed up." He nodded toward the refrigerator. "Now I'm ready for a beer."

I brought it to him, still unsettled by a need for answers. "I wish you'd tell me more about her, Dad. What she was like, I mean."

He held out his hand to me, the gesture vaguely menacing. I put my hand reluctantly in his. "All right, look, girl. *I* decide what is best for you to know." He was squeezing my hand now, but it was not yet painful. "You have to trust me."

His choice of the word trust inflamed me. "I miss her, Dad. And sometimes . . ."

"What?" His grip tightened. "Sometimes what?"

"I just get that feeling—how you don't like me to feel. You know . . . like before."

"What the *hell* are you talking about?" He couldn't say

it, not the actual words, but the alarm in his face told me he knew.

Committed to my course now, I went on. "That bad feeling."

He looked disgusted. "Not that sick stuff, you mean. That sick stuff with the knife."

I looked away from him. "I can't help it. Sometimes I get lonely. Too lonely. 'Cause everything would have been all right, if . . ."

"Oh, shit! Just say it!"

"If I hadn't killed her."

He freed my hand abruptly. "You never killed her! What a goddamn crazy way to put it. She just died when you were born."

"I know, Dad. Toxemia. My poison."

He gulped his beer. "Don't talk like that, Carla. Christ—see how you are. Anything to ruin my mood. Anything to get to me."

I knew he was right. "Sorry, Dad. I just got to thinking about how she died."

He grimaced. "Why the hell can't you ever think about the good things?"

"But I do," I said. "I think about how it was with the other one. Mrs. Andrews." Ignoring the look on his face, I pressed on. "She always talked so funny, remember?"

He belched elaborately. "I told you before. She couldn't speak English worth a damn."

"I remember her calling me Carlek."

"Some nickname. That's all."

I envied him suddenly, that he was an adult when he knew her, that he could remember Mrs. Andrews clearly.

"I've told you a hundred times. You stayed with her for a few months while I was traveling on that job."

I astonished myself by saying quietly, "I want to see her again."

He made a waggish face at me. "You're nuts—you really are. She's all the way down in San Diego somewhere. If she's still there even. And she'd never remember you."

But I thought: She will. She does. And I knew it in my soul, Jessie. Because once she held me in her arms. She kissed me. She sang to me.

He crumpled the empty beer can in one hand. "I thought you wanted to talk about Jeannie anyway. Not this one."

"Oh, yes, Dad. Yes, please."

"All right then." He was smug with power. "All right. First off, she was the best-looking girl in the senior class. In the whole school for that matter. Hell—in the whole fucking town. *Everybody* wanted to date Jeanne Mallory."

"And you were the captain of the football team."

"Damn right I was. Except that the old man managed to pooh-pooh even that."

"You were the best-looking guy in school, weren't you."

He gave me a knowing look. "Oh, it's flattery, is it?" But I knew from the hint of Irish brogue he threw in that he wasn't objecting.

"You were, Daddy. Weren't you?"

His eyes were clear blue and dreamy now. "I guess I wasn't so bad. At least she didn't think so. And when they crowned her Homecoming Queen I was right there beside her. The night of that dance was our night. After they came in—Jeannie and her court—she and I had to dance out there in front of everybody. Nobody else but the two of us." Without apparent thought my father went to the refrigerator then and took out his own can of beer. "She was there at the awards banquet, too, when I got the most valuable player trophy. Jay and Jeannie. Jay

82

Hughes and Jeannie Mallory. We were *it*, Carly. That whole school respected us."

He sat down again. "Would you believe the old man tried to queer *that* one for me, too? And that was it for me. That was it!" He took a deep drink of beer, then set the can down hard on the table. "Said things. Always did have an evil tongue. Things about me. And it got to old man Mallory. Shit." He scowled suddenly. "What the bloody hell are we talking about this for anyway? It's fucking over with. Done."

"I know, Dad."

The pain in his expression unnerved me.

"I just don't like this bullshit conversation anymore."

"Okay." I took a long, deep breath. "But I have to ask you one more thing, Dad. Please? I mean, I just want to know if you hold it against me. Because of my mother. And what happened."

He closed his eyes for a moment. "Hell, no."

I wanted to believe him, Jessie. I wanted to, but still, I couldn't.

He was crumpling the second beer can. "Forget it. Let's just get to bed."

I went upstairs then and lay down on my sleeping bag. I could hear him moving about the house, closing windows and locking the doors.

Then I could hear his footsteps coming up the stairs. They stopped at my bedroom doorway. "How can you sleep like that? Jesus."

I looked up at him. He was unbuttoning his shirt.

"On the floor like that. With all your clothes on."

I gave him the answer I have always given him. "I don't know. I guess I just like to." Because I couldn't tell him the truth, about how I feel safer this way.

He took off his shirt and draped it over one arm. "Get up here now and give your old man a kiss."

I got up slowly—wondering. Thinking: It can go either way.

Then, standing next to him, I knew. When he pulled me close and said, "Who cares about her anyway? We don't want her, baby." And he was moving against me. "Oh, yeah," he said huskily. "We have each other now. And that's all we need."

Mama, I wake up and the air is all gone from me and the nightmonster says, What a little flirty girl, and he takes off my nightie and feels me all over and then he says, I have something for you, and he makes my head go down by the loggie and says, lick it, and the loggie gets too big and I can't get air in me and the sticky stuff comes out and he pushes down my face and says, Here, Goldilocks, it's your porridge. And his hand is all over my head and after it hurts where I swallow and the air goes all away and it gets black. . . .

"Look!" He is grasping my ankle.

I open my eyes to find his accusing forefinger pressed against my thigh. And he is staring at the cuts there; narrow red lines oozing now.

"What's that?"

But even as he asks it, he knows.

"I told you, Dad. It's that feeling . . ."

His grip loosens around my ankle. He lifts his other hand and presses his fingers hard into his eyelids. "It's just to hurt me."

"No." He is wrong about this and I want to explain. "No. It's so nothing worse will happen." His mouth gapes and I look into his tired eyes. "Sometimes—I have to."

He releases my ankle now and pulls away. "What do you want? Want me to quit drinking? Is that it? Okay. I'll quit drinking." His lower lip trembles unexpectedly. "Everything I do is for you, baby. Don't you know that? You're my whole life."

"I know, Dad."

He glances down at my leg again. "I guess it isn't that bad though. Is it?"

"Oh, no," I tell him, and it's true.

"I'll get a washcloth."

His offer touches me. "No. I can do it, Dad."

And then he is lying down again, pulling the big pillow up between his knees. He doesn't seem angry anymore, or even sad. And soon he is asleep.

I stay there for a long time watching him. And from his parted lips comes a gentle, even sound that is not quite snoring. His dark blond eyelashes are serene against his cheek, and near his face his big open hand lies as vulnerable as a baby's. Except for one pale foot, his lower body has managed to find sanctuary beneath the dark blue sheet. And before I know what I am doing, I lean forward to adjust the cover so that it conceals and warms that errant foot.

Oh, my father. At this moment I could almost think you are what you seem to be.

A good man.

A good man sleeping the merciful sleep of the just.

So it's over.

I'm warm again under my quilt and nothing more will happen tonight.

I am grateful, Jessie, for this moment.

Because, as it says in the Bible, to the hungry soul, every bitter thing is sweet.

Three

___

YOUR TIME GROWS SHORT, *my father.*

You lie before me, deathlike in your stupor, but I take no risks. Patient and watchful, I remain firmly connected with your gun.

The stench in this room sickens me, its familiarity making it no less odious. Booze and semen and urine (because your drinking long ago crippled your bladder) and sweat. The smells, you told me once, of a man.

Yes. And since it is I who change your sheets, I am aware of the spreading stains on your mattress. Those foul discolorations are as well known to me as the expressions on your face. Once, when I was little and even more fanciful than I am now, I remember pulling off your sheets while they were still damp with our secretions, convinced I would find a new stain there made in my own likeness. A fitting self-portrait.

For I am guilty as charged, my father.

Of incest.

From the Latin word incestus—impure.

Somehow I could smell the meaning of that word for years before I knew its definition.

Which brings me to another of your mistakes. Or perhaps you would call it a calculated risk. A gamble that contained the slowly germinating seeds of your destruction.

Sister Mary Paul. Teacher and Catholic nun. Sister Mary Paul—tiny, winsome and surpassingly holy.

Another bold stroke, my father, to be sure. Your enrolling me in the fifth grade at Saint Agatha's School. How the irony of that must have warmed you over your evening toddies.

As for me, the doltish ten-year-old, I soon believed I had received nothing less than the pearl of great price. The wisdom valued above rubies. Because Sister Mary Paul put into my hands the key to the mystery of life itself. Unveiled a new world peopled with apostles and martyrs and saints. Unfolded refinements in the art of sacrifice, the joys of suffering.

Suddenly my own plight was illuminated with meaning. The purpose of my misery was to win grace, an ethereal substance that would flow into my soul until my death. Then my spiritual account, enriched by the fruits of my immolation, would insure my eternal relief.

In my ignorance, I even came to imagine the possibility of leading a sanctified life. And I developed what Sister Mary Paul termed a special devotion to the Blessed Mother.

That Mother most pure. Most chaste. That Mother undefiled. I said the words over and over again, my father. But, dull-witted as always, I failed to grasp them.

Yet, kneeling in the wax and incense peace before the statue of the Virgin, I was increasingly admired by Sister Mary Paul. And soon she was talking of my future— First Communion, then Confirmation, and one day perhaps a still higher vocation. To follow in her own hallowed footsteps.

Holy Mother of God. Vessel of Honor. Holy Virgin of Virgins. My joy exceeded understanding; my path was set. Not only was there meaning in my life now, but a virtuous cause.

Obsessed with the craving to be worthy, I haunted the church.

Do you remember, my father? Because you found me there one afternoon, and before I could think better of it, I was blurting out my ultimate dream: to become a nun.

Your look of shock was quickly succeeded by your laughter echoing lewdly through the church. Beguiled as you were by this crowning irony, you were barely able to regain your self-control.

I still remember the "enlightment" of the lecture that followed—not your words really, or even their general meaning, but the tone of it all, the unsuppressed merriment in your eyes, the mockery in your voice. Indeed, ridicule proved a most effective tool in bringing your presumptuous child back into the real world.

Underscored that night when the unspeakable happened again. To provide me with the final monstrous proof of what I am. And forcing me to compare myself with my mentor—Sister Mary Paul. Teacher and Catholic nun. Virginal and pure. Free from stain. Inviolate vessel of honor. Singular vessel of devotion.

When you came home early that next morning, you found me again, didn't you, my father? On the floor in the dark bedroom. Discovered your daughter who, in her ignorance of more efficacious methods, had attempted to thrust our dullest kitchen knife into her heart.

Jessie, you're frustrated with me now, more than ever before.

And you're angry.

You try, but you don't understand. Not about Emily, and not about me.

What you want to know is why.

Why Emily always wore white and lived her whole life in that prison.

Why I remain in this sad, lonely house with my father.

If I told you the worst thing is having nowhere to turn, you would come forward eagerly. "Not so," you would say. I can turn to you, Jessie. Call you on the telephone. Pour out my story.

Then I can go to the police and tell them what happens to me.

Talk my head off.

Most important of all, I can refuse to go home again.

And it would be over for you. Your part completed. Your job well done.

But what would happen then? To me? I don't know how to live on my own. I'm not independent the way Dean is.

And who would want me?

I've just read it over, Jessie. Everything I've written to you. And it's no wonder that you're angry.

That you hope this long sadistic waste I call my life can change.

But for me escape is an illusion.

If I went away, my father would search for me until he found me.

I belong to him.

I am his life.

Oh, God.

I feel so weak and ill.

As you discount what I say with the shrug of your shoulder.

Forgetting that if I told my story, the most likely prospect is that no one would believe it.

At times I am unsure of it myself. Perhaps what I describe is nothing more than a hallucination.

Remember the philospher who said that what we call reality may only be a dream? I could be a dreamer, Jessie, and this a nightmare filled with specters all my own.

In short, I have no proof.

All right then. I surrender to your judgment.

The truth is that I can work myself up into a frenzy of contempt for my father, plan for his sweetly slow and agonizing death. And then something always sidles in, something corrosive to my resolve: hope. The thing with feathers that perches in the soul. Hope that it is there after all inside him. What I long for.

No—I dare not call it love.

But perhaps the possibility. Of love.

Jessie. You do not give up.

You never stop urging me to believe in myself.

And assuring me that I am not alone.

I have no quarrel with your compassion, or even your good intentions. Only with your ignorance.

My confinement is solitary.

What can I expect from the world—my gentle, patient Jessie—if even you don't understand?

Do you really think I have not been down the path your mind is taking now? I have already done what you are asking. Or tried to do it.

When I was younger.

In fact, I can even remember when it was. In the seventh grade—my third year at Saint Agatha's. Have I mentioned that in the process of selling Monsignor Dailey a set of encyclopedias, my father had agreed to send me to a Catholic school?

Before my first year was over there, Jessie, I knew I didn't belong. Not that I didn't admire the nuns, but when they talked about sin they were referring to the telling of little white lies or the theft of penny candy. They didn't have the least idea of what sin really is.

At the beginning of the seventh grade, Sister Marietta introduced herself to our class by describing the saint for whom she was named—Saint Marietta, whom most people call Maria Goretti. One of the most beloved saints of the Church, she told us proudly, and only twelve (the age of most of us seventh graders) when she died.

When our teacher began to tell us Maria's story, I could actually see it—the little country village in Italy, the saintly child attending daily Mass and Holy Communion.

Enter Allesandro. A teenage boy with sins of the flesh on his mind.

Sister Marietta looked at us solemnly, as nuns do when they bring up anything related to sex. "Allesandro asked Maria to sin with him," she said, "but Maria was already known throughout Nettuno for her holiness. And, of course, she refused."

My stomach lurched with nausea, and certain that I could predict the outcome, I knew I wanted no more of this story.

But Sister Marietta's pale face was glowing with a strange eagerness. "Allesandro went on insisting, boys and girls, revealing his evil plans to Maria. Then he threatened her with his knife." The nun's eyes scanned the classroom carefully. When she spoke again, her voice was triumphant. "And Maria *still* said no!"

Feeling an evil taste rising in my throat, I put my hand

over my mouth. At that moment I hated my teacher for telling this story, which she so cruelly prolonged.

"Tearfully, she told Allesandro again—no," said Sister Marietta. "Then he stabbed her. Not once, boys and girls, but many times. Yet even as the life drained out of her small body, she repeated that word to him again and again—no."

A boy near me snickered and Sister glared in our direction; a moment later her beatific expression reappeared. "Now I will read to you from the special parts of the Mass in honor of Saint Maria Goretti:

'Come, spouse of Christ, receive the crown which the Lord hath prepared for thee forever: for the love of whom thou didst shed thy blood . . . he that loveth his life shall lose it, he that hateth his life in this world keepeth it until life eternal. Deliver not to the vulture the life of thy dove . . . We offer you, Lord, this appeasing sacrifice by which your blessed handmaid Mary, already in her first youth, learned to offer you her body as a holy and pleasing victim. Grant we pray you, Lord, to those whom you have already refreshed with heavenly bread, the same fortitude in defending their chastity of body and soul which you have wonderfully bestowed upon your handmaiden Mary.' "

Chastity. Virginity. Everyday words at Saint Agatha's, Jessie, and I'd already looked them up. *Virgin:* a person, especially a young woman, who has never had sexual intercourse. *Intercourse:* the sexual joining of two individuals. *Join:* to bring or come together; connect; unite.

I didn't know, Jessie, cretin that I was, until I heard another girl talking. Didn't know that virginity was about a thing inside you that would bleed if you lost it. A thing, Lena Miller told an excited group of girls, that was somewhere in your "pee-pee hole."

Then I understood. Because I'd bled from there many times.

When I looked at Sister Marietta's flushed face that day, I finally made the connection, realized with horror that I was not a virgin. And it didn't matter how much I prayed. I had nothing left to defend.

Then, as if reading my mind, Sister Marietta closed her missal and explained that if any one of us gave up our lives in defense of Christ or any Christian virtue, such as chastity, all our sins would be immediately forgiven. No matter how many sins were on our soul and no matter how terrible they were, we would go straight to heaven.

A new interpretation of my life emerged with enticing clarity. It was simple: all along the answer was supposed to be no. Without regard for the consequences. The reason I continued to suffer was that up to now I hadn't been truly ready to die. Suicide, of course, didn't count because it was a mortal sin. But it suddenly burst upon me that I could die in another way, without sin, and be rewarded for it: if someone else killed me. As long as I died defending myself against another's desecration.

Trembling with relief, Jessie, I wondered why I had never seen this before. Why I had not learned, had not been willing to assume my destiny as "an appeasing sacrifice, a holy and pleasing victim." While all the time, back at Saint Agatha's Church, the smiling Madonna in her blue and white robes had been waiting for me. To fight back. Yes, to fight my father to the death.

And it might not even matter then about my not being a virgin. Hadn't Sister Marietta said so? Because after I died all my sins would be forgiven.

When I got home from school I lay down on my bedroom floor and wept with joy.

Soon, I told the Blessed Mother. Mother most pure. Mother most chaste. Tower of ivory. House of gold.

I will come to you soon.
Maybe even tonight.

Ironically, my father stayed out so late that night that he came home too tired to hurt me.

The next day at lunchtime I went into the church and knelt down before the statue of the Madonna and she talked to me. Her lips didn't move, but I heard her clearly in my head. And her voice was like yours, Jessie—melodious and serene. She said that I was not to be afraid and there was a place for me in heaven. That when I came to her she would put her arm around my shoulder. She would shelter me under her long blue cloak and we would always be together.

As soon as my sins were washed away.

She told me to remember how her Son had suffered on His holy cross. How He was laid in her arms after the death of His human body. How He had won eternal life for all human souls who followed Him. She told me that He would help me just as He had helped Maria.

I knelt there in the silent church drawing strength from the flicker of the sanctuary lamp.

And I knew it would be soon. Unless, of course, there was a miracle. That the Blessed Virgin would somehow touch the soul of my father. Transform him into someone else. Yet how could I ask her for so much? The sin that had already taken place warranted a minimum sentence of death.

That night I listened for my father for hours. Then, just as fatigue was engulfing me, I saw him standing beside my bed.

"Carly?"

I didn't move, thinking how unexpected it always seemed. That it would be better to lie still and wait.

He held out his hand. "I know you're awake now. Come on."

From deep inside myself I summoned the word—no. While the sound of it was loud in my head, it was too difficult to say.

He grabbed me by the shoulders. "What's wrong with you?"

"No," I said finally. Weakly.

"What the hell are you talking about?" Shock in his voice, his big fingers grinding into my shoulders. "You come on!"

This time I shook my head, but my teeth were chattering and I thought: I'm such a coward. Maria wouldn't have been like this.

He threw me back onto the bed and shook his finger at me. "Get up right now, you little slut. I don't feel like playing games."

I was afraid to die, but I needed to die. I tried to ask the Blessed Mother to help me.

But he did something he'd never done before. He lay down right beside me on the canopy bed. And it was crowded because his body was much too big. His breath was sour and he pressed his forefinger and thumb into my cheeks and pulled my face up until my nose was nearly touching his.

"What's wrong with you? What're you trying to do to me?"

Should I tell him now about the plan? How much I need to die?

He released my face and moved his hand into my pajama bottoms, saying, "If you don't get up right now, I'm going to make you scream."

I could feel what he was going to do with his fingers and I knew it was a sin so I slipped away from him and off my bed. I ran into the closet.

Coward, I told myself, still trying to concentrate on the Blessed Mother. But I could see at last that it wasn't going to be easy. To die.

He pulled open the door of the closet and now he was smiling. "I know what's wrong with you, Carly. You're not in the mood yet. But I can fix that." He took my arm and pulled me easily out of the closet. My legs were so wobbly I fell, and then he picked me up and carried me into his bedroom. He held me so close I could feel his heart thudding and mine, too, and I thought: It will happen soon now. It will all be over.

He lay me down on his bed and told me not to move. Then he opened the bottom drawer of his bureau and took out a shoe box and set it on the bed beside me like a gift. "Sometimes ladies aren't in the right mood," said my father and he was breathing fast and his mouth was curled up a little on one side. He took the lid off the shoe box and pulled me up so I was sitting and brought out some pictures to show me.

I can't tell you what was in the pictures, Jessie, but they were of grownups and little kids.

"See, Carly? These kids all know what to do, don't they? They're smiling, too. They're having a great time."

Something about the pictures made me want to scream. He stared at them for a while and his eyes got glassy. Then he looked at me and his hand was moving fast on himself, and then he put his other hand in my pajama bottoms and said, "Are you in the mood now?"

I knew it was time to say no again, but my throat was frozen. I could only move my lips. I was looking at the pictures and thinking: My father is telling the truth. Other kids have to do this, too.

Then he said, "You know, Carly, tonight could be real special for us." And he pushed me back down and the pillow came up over my face a little and I couldn't see very well. He said, "You're twelve now. It's time for you to become a real woman."

At first I thought my father could make me start to menstruate like some of the other girls in my class.

Then he was on top of me, like lots of times before, only this time he was trying to push his penis into me and I forgot to say no because I was screaming and he put the pillow over my head and let if off again just before I was going to faint.

Then it was all messy on my legs and there was an awful burning place between them and I knew for sure I had to die.

His whole face was smiling now. "God, that was good, baby. Fantastic!"

And I said, "No," really loud. And then I started to scream again and he slapped me hard. "Stop that!" He put his hand over my mouth. "You aren't that hurt."

When he took his hand off, I said, "I have to die."

He just shook his head like he didn't understand, and then he laughed a little. "You're crazy."

"I have to die, Daddy. Please."

He looked at me and then he pulled my pajama bottoms up again, right over the sticky mess on me. "You want me to *kill* you?"

I said yes. I felt brave now. It hurt so much inside me that the best thing I could think of was to sleep forever.

"Why?" he asked.

"So I can go to heaven."

He looked at me curiously for a while, and then he said, "Who's feeding you that, Carla? The nuns? Yeah, of course. But there is no heaven, girl. No hell either. All that stuff is bullshit."

I closed my eyes.

"Look—don't start buying all that religious crap.

Think of it as a fairy story, okay? 'Cause none of it is true."

But even that didn't matter anymore. "I need to die," I said again.

He looked puzzled. "Why?"

"'Cause of the way you hurt me."

His face got red then, and he jerked his thumb toward the pictures spread out on the big bed. "How come they don't look hurt then? Huh, Carla? Your problem is you just don't relax. Your mother was the same fucking way. But you'll learn. I can give you everything you need."

Even surer now, I said it once more. "I need to die, Daddy." I wanted to put my hand down there on me because it hurt so much. But I couldn't do it in front of him because I knew he would say something ugly, or else try to hurt me again.

"You know what, kid? You're crazy, same as she was."

"I'm going to die, Daddy. If there's no mortal sin, I can."

"What're you talking about?" He cleared his throat. "You'd better not try anything like that again."

"Yes, I can." Right then I was hating him so hard I thought the feeling might kill us both. I found myself wanting to crush his face and gouge out his eyes and knead the pulp that was left in my bare hands. "I can kill myself if I want to."

He frowned. "Oh, no, you don't. No more crazy stunts."

I was surprised by sudden tears. "You hurt me too much."

And then I saw a wondrous thing, Jessie. I saw tears in *his* eyes. For the first time I could ever remember. "Hey, baby, you can't die on me," he said. "You're my baby." Then he took me in his arms in this tender way and held me close. "I need you, Carly. I live for you."

He was holding me so tight it was hard to breathe, but

I didn't struggle. This mood of his was new; it melted me. "I want to get you a present, baby. Anything you want. Your birthday's coming up, but I don't mean that. A special present for right now. For my little woman."

And there it was, Jessie. What I hadn't expected.

Didn't I tell you about my stupidity? And, yes, the vile and distressing photographs were still spread out on the bed, the two of us still wrapped together in the deadly smell and feel of his semen, pain thrusting like a dagger between my legs.

Yet he had me.

There would be no death after all.

My father told me he'd pick me up the next day after school and we'd go downtown for ice cream and I could pick out a wonderful present.

Only it hurt too much to walk the next day, so I stayed home from school.

And when I did go back, I talked to Sister Marietta, tried to question her about the story she'd told us.

It happened at recess time. "Was that story like an example?" I asked her.

Sister Marietta was watching the far side of the playground. "What do you mean?"

"Like the examples Monsignor Dailey gives us sometimes? They're to teach us something, but they didn't really happen?"

"Oh, no," said Sister. "The story of Maria Goretti is true. That's how she became a saint."

"But when Maria died she wasn't *still* a virgin."

Sister was looking uncomfortable now. Nuns get embarrassed pretty easily. "Of course, she was, Carla."

"But he was so much bigger than her," I explained.

She nodded. "Three years older, too."

"Then he must have . . . " I hesitated. Was I going too far?

"Must have what, Carla?"

"He must have just done it to her."

Sister was leaning down closer to me now. "Maria said no."

"But that doesn't matter," I said.

She took one of my hands in hers. "What?"

"Sister—he never had to ask her or anything. It was—up to him."

A tiny frown came into her face. "I've told you how it happened."

I was very patient. "But, Sister, saying no doesn't matter."

Her eyes, which were naturally kind of round, had a surprised look.

"She tried her best," I added. "But it was easy for him."

Sister Marietta's eyes looked like they were going to pop out.

For some reason, I could feel myself relaxing a little. "I mean, she tried all she could. But he didn't kill her because she said no." I smiled at her, hoping it would make her feel better.

Sister's hand felt cold in mine. "Then why?"

I searched for the right words and when I found them, I said, "Because he wanted to."

Sister Marietta released my hand. She looked sick, Jessie. And just now, remembering it this way, I realize that she probably wanted to ask me. But she just couldn't bring herself to say the words:

Carla, how do you know?

Mama, we're waiting at the very top of the Cyclone Racer and we start to come down only then it gets soft underneath us and I see I'm flying all alone in the sky and

100

it gets darker and then I see the face as big as the whole ocean and I am only a speck and I can see his tongue and the way the nightmonster is laughing and he is getting closer and I scream out, *don't come!* but I can't help it, Mama, I fly right into his mouth!

Dearest Jessie.

I am very tired. I had a nightmare last night and slept only fitfully this morning.

After sixth period today, my counselor asked me to come to her office. Until then, I'd thought of Mrs. Forsythe as a sweet but gullible old lady who'd believe anything I chose to tell her. She's a small woman, even shorter than I am, and round as a dumpling. Like my own Leona Ly, Mrs. Forsythe gives the impression that if you hugged her, you'd melt right into her.

"Now here we are," she said after she'd located my school records, and she began to read. I could just imagine what she was finding there: words like *introvert* . . . *loner* . . . *misfit*.

Pursing her lips a little, she said, "You've moved several times." News to her, of course, but hardly to me. Counselors always try to sound as though they're enlightening you on the subject of yourself.

Touching at her hair with a delicate little-girl gesture, Mrs. Forsythe read on. And I couldn't help noticing the framed photograph on her desk of a man with sparse white hair, pinkish skin and the benevolent look of a rabbit. A man who matched Mrs. Forsythe to perfection.

She removed her half-glasses and fixed unexpectedly intelligent eyes on mine. "Carla, you look very tired."

"I'm working on a term paper. Last night I just forgot about the time."

"You always look tired," she said. "Exhausted really."

I pointed unnecessarily at my cheekbones. "It's the circles. A hereditary thing. Deep circles. And nothing seems to help." This explanation has served me well during my school years because most counselors hesitate to criticize a student's genes.

Mrs. Forsythe's gaze, though kind, was perceptive. "Do bloodshot eyes run in your family, too?" She paused. "I read here that at Alvarado you fainted twice last year."

I dragged in another of my old standbys: "I'm anemic." But my tongue stumbled guiltily over the word. "I'm taking iron tablets."

"Even now?" she asked shrewdly.

I was beginning to feel genuinely uneasy. It was clear that Mrs. Forsythe isn't the kind of counselor you can satisfy with a two-minute summation of your life.

"I don't want to pry," she said with exasperating patience. "But I've been in education for over thirty years now. I'd be pretty dense if I hadn't picked up a few instincts along the way."

A frantic light in my brain signaled danger.

"I think you're in trouble—though I don't know what kind." She paused suggestively, but I let the silence widen between us, feeling that would be more effective than a denial. "Drugs can do this to a student," she went on. "Or working long hours after school at a job. Some students do that, I know. Some have to, of course." She paused again. "I just want you to know I'm here, Carla. This is my last year working with young people. And even though I'm a grandmother, I don't shock easily. You can tell me anything."

Almost anything, I amended silently. I also decided, reluctantly, that I liked her. Admired her even. Which is all the more reason to avoid her completely.

Mrs. Forsythe massaged the bridge of her nose, replaced her glasses, and looked down again at my folder.

"You're more than bright, Carla. And your grades are consistently good. But the classes you take aren't challenging enough. Your I.Q. puts you in the superior category. You really belong in our honors program." She looked up at me again. "Have you considered that?"

I shrugged my indifference. Because I don't want the honors program, Jessie. It's harder to remain anonymous in those smaller classes, and the kids have to work too hard. I couldn't possibly muster up that kind of energy, "superior" I.Q. or not.

"It's an outside job, isn't it?" Mrs. Forsythe asked slyly. "A night job?"

An impulsive laughter, touched with hysteria, rose within me. I had to bite my tongue, fight off the urge to lay everything out for her then and there. A night job. Certainly, Mrs. Forsythe. I am a night worker. I make myself useful during the long hours when the rest of the world is sleeping.

I shook my head, but an odd chuckling sound escaped me in the process.

"Drugs," said Mrs. Forsythe sadly; it wasn't a question.

I struggled desperately for composure because all at once I was breathless with rage. And fighting the urge to grab her by those round complacent shoulders and shake her till her dentures rattled. Yearning suddenly to overpower her, to crush her soft shapeless body beneath my own.

And I'm not even sure why.

Unaware of her peril, Mrs. Forsythe gave me a final appealing look and repeated her offer to listen, her willingness to advise me at any time. Then she was prudent enough to let me go.

Drugs, Jessie. Imagine. She probably thinks I spend my nights getting high on pot or shooting heroin. But drugs—for recreation—are unthinkable for me.

Stay alert is my motto; stay alive.

I do not intend to die by chance.

Not that drugs don't have their purposes, of course. Like the pain pills and barbiturates I've gradually spirited away from my father's medicine cabinet. The little bundle I keep hidden so ingeniously in Mymouse's pert gray head.

My death insurance, so to speak.

And an occasional aspirin can be helpful, too, at times, don't you think? And certainly the little pill I take most mornings of every month.

You know the one I mean, Jessie.

The tiny one that comes in the circular package. My wheel of protection.

Of course.

The one that keeps my father and me from begetting a monster.

Magic, Jessie!

This very day I received a letter from Dean.

Drawn on the front of the note paper are two ripe red strawberries—because he knows how much I love them—and he writes:

Dear Carla,

It's been a century since we've seen each other. I worry about you and keep hoping things are going okay there. I sure have missed you, especially with your birthday and all. Don't worry. I didn't forget.

So you're seventeen now. It isn't rocking chair time yet, but you have to start planning for the future. That's all I think about myself these days and I have an idea for both of us. I can't wait to tell you.

Unfortunately, my new school is basically boring. The journalism class isn't half as good as the one at Alvarado. I mean, the teacher is completely ridiculous. Things just aren't the same for me anymore, and I'm lonely as hell without you.

But I saved the good news for last. Our houseparent, Sid, the only good thing about my life now, is lending me his van on Saturday so I can come and see you. What if we meet at the library near your house (if I can find it all right) about three? Then we'll have the van all to ourselves for a couple of hours before I have to head back.

I'll call you Friday night to see if the time is okay. I'll use that same signal of ringing twice first, then hanging up and calling back, like we did before.

One more hot flash: this year I earned enough money to buy you a real birthday present.

Hurry up, Saturday.

     Love,
     Dean

I drifted through my chores this afternoon in a euphoric haze. Because I still don't believe it, that Dean really does miss me and that Saturday we will actually be together again.

It may sound foolish, Jessie, but at this moment I feel something in common with all the world's lovers. The ones I know, at least, the ones in books. And I must admit I have always yearned to feel what they feel.

And now I am Levin, floating through the early morning streets to Kitty's house in *Anna Karenina*. Everything looks as new to me, and as movingly beautiful.

I am Mattie Silver, who doesn't even feel the biting cold on that steep wintry hillside; those are my lips sweeping over the face of Ethan Frome.

And I am as astonished as Jane Eyre when her proud Rochester finally pours out his heart of love to her.

Please don't laugh at these effusions, Jessie. It's just that all I can think of now is him. Images—held back from me before by pain—crowd exultantly into my mind.

And suddenly I remember the feel of warm sand and the vigor of the surf one glorious day last spring.

Easter vacation. When Dean convinced me to take yet another precarious step into my future. Though if my father hadn't been at an all-day realtors' meeting, I would never have been so brave.

Dean was the Pied Piper enticing me to take a bus with him to the beach. I hadn't ridden on one since I was little, and the experience was oddly comforting. It was as though the big warm bus was a congenial place my father could never invade.

Of course, it was still difficult to overcome my paranoia about his finding out. When I was little my father always told me that whether he was with me or not, he could see what I was doing. I was such a dumb kid I believed this for years, and crazy as it sounds, I think I still do. At least a little.

But that day I put these thoughts away from me and the next thing I knew, Dean and I were standing knee deep in the water at Belmont Shore, clinging to each other and laughing like any other kids in the world.

Then we were lying down on the beach, and I was savoring the unexpected riches to be found in an April day. And I can remember wondering if this was the joy most people come to know. Is life usually made up of such enchanted things, Jessie? I hope it is—especially yours.

Because for that day I was really a part of life. Not just an observer, but an authentic player in the drama.

It seemed so extraordinary to be lying there with Dean, our bodies prone and vulnerable, to be breathing in the damp salt air and listening to the whoosh of the surf. Our faces were only a few inches apart and he gently stroked my arm. "This is great," he said.

"I know."

He smiled. "I have good ideas, don't I?"

"Yes."

And then he said it. I wasn't prepared at all, but he actually said, "I love you."

I couldn't reply.

"I know I'm not—you know—right. I mean, like other guys or whatever. I get pretty confused sometimes. My feelings. But it still seems right to say it. I love you."

But why? I couldn't understand how he could love me. I looked away from him then because all at once I was feeling a chill. I closed my eyes, but I could still see a man's naked back, his hand on a doorknob, and a little girl—her body raw with pain and fatigue—on the bed behind him. Calling him back for a moment and the man turning around as she says, "Daddy? Is this like love?" And he says, "Sure, baby. Sure."

"Why?" I asked Dean now. *Why do you love me?*

His fingers played lightly on my shoulder. "You're my only true friend."

Tears sprang into my eyes.

"I have to tell you something though. Well—you might not understand it either. But I'm not sure—you know—about doing things. You know?"

I nodded.

He was looking uncomfortable. "And there's something else I have to tell you. About somebody at school. How I feel and all."

With those words came my first pang of jealousy, surprising and insistent. And I saw then what the Bible meant: jealousy as strong as death, as hard as hell.

"Not another kid," he said awkwardly. Then he cleared his throat. "It's Mr. Freed."

Curiously relieved, I listened as he told me more about it, about loving his journalism teacher. And it sounded a lot like the way I love you, Jessie, and the way I loved

Sister Mary Paul. But to Dean it seemed to bring only pain.

"Aaron J. Freed—that's his full name. He's in his late twenties I guess. And I just like the way he *is*," Dean said. "And I respect him, you know? He's fair about stuff, really an honest type. He always says integrity is the most important thing a journalist can have. He worked for the *Washington Post* once." Dean hesitated. "This one day when he was looking over one of my paste-ups, he was standing really close to me and I—I . . ."

Wanting to help him, I didn't know how.

He stiffened a little. "Not that I wanted to feel that way or anything. I'd rather be like other guys. I guess. I'm not sure yet. I mean, I can put on the act sometimes. It's easy to know what's expected—that's for sure. It's all most guys my age even talk about. The contest or whatever. The race. 'What'd you do? How far did you get? Are you there yet?' Just one goal really: to get the girls in bed." He frowned. "I just couldn't be like that. No matter who I was attracted to—"

"We could do it," I offered. "If you want to."

"Huh?"

"It doesn't matter that much," I said. But I could see that I'd spoken out of turn, that I'd shocked him.

"It does to me." His eyes darkened. "With love it does."

I looked away. What audacity, I told myself, to think Dean would ever want me. "Forget it," I said. "I'm too ugly."

He looked startled. "Stop it. You're not ugly. You're like—a little bird. Sometimes I'd just like to take care of you forever."

"I'm nothing," I told him. "Anybody's better than me." I gave him a bold look, not caring about risk now. "And I'm numb."

"Carla, why are you acting like this?"

"I don't know."

"It started out good today."

I kept the silence of the guilty.

"You've done this other times, too," he said, his anger building. "It's like you can't stand it when we start to feel a little close."

"But it's true."

"What?"

"What I said before. If I'm not too ugly for you. We can do it."

He rolled away from me. "God."

The silence lengthened between us, and the great expanse of sky was suddenly overwhelming to me. "I'm ruining things, aren't I?"

He turned back to me again, and I couldn't bear the look in his eyes. "Yeah."

It was true, but I didn't know why. I only knew that I'd offended him and that I must try to find an explanation.

Just then Emily, my precious Emily, came to my rescue. And I quoted, " 'The plenty hurt me, 'twas so new, Myself felt ill and odd.' "

When Dean didn't respond, I went on. "Emily Dickinson. It's from a poem of hers that I never used to understand. Not till I met you anyway. Want to hear a little?"

He nodded dubiously.

> " 'I had been hungry all the years;
> My noon had come to dine;
> I, trembling, drew the table near,
> And touched the curious wine.
>
> . . .
>
> The plenty hurt me, 'twas so new,
> Myself felt ill and odd,

As berry of a mountain bush
Transplanted to the road.' "

I really did grasp the poem now, but Dean didn't. "Tell me again," he said. "Only in your own words this time."

But I knew if Emily couldn't make him see it, it was futile for me to try. I looked down at my watch. "What time is the next bus?"

"God, you're frustrating," he said. "How can anyone be so sensitive and so *in*sensitive at the same time?"

"What do you mean?"

"Carla, what you said before—about us. It means a lot to me that you might want to. But I just don't know what it means to you. The way you talk about it, I guess."

At first his innocence was touching; then depression stole over me. "I don't know. You wouldn't like me."

"Carla," he said then, and his arm was suddenly around me, urging me closer.

My embrace of him was tense, uncertain. "I'm sorry."

And we didn't speak again for a long time, the two of us somehow encapsulated now in our own private space. He seemed so small in my arms and I could feel the whole length of his body, the pounding heart of the surf underneath us.

Then I was seeing another boy. And remembering running barefoot with him along the lacy edge of another shore, while the Cyclone Racer loomed above us in the shimmering summer heat.

Another life, Jessie, from long ago.

When I was safe with Broder, as now I was safe with Dean.

Safe with Dean.
For awhile.
Until suspicion took hold of him.

It happened near the end of the school year, near the end of our time together. We were in the Community Room at the library after school, and Dean was helping me set up for a performance.

When we were ready, he decided he wanted to talk to Mymouse.

Concerned about how late it was, I said, "You can't talk to Max now."

Dean raised his all-too-familiar eyebrow. "Max?"

"No," I said quickly. "I mean Mymouse."

"Is his real name Max?"

I shook my head.

"I'll ask him," Dean said. "All right, Mymouse, what's the story?"

My puppet didn't answer.

Dean looked back at me. "It seems to be harder for Mymouse to lie than for you. He probably knows he can trust me."

"I do," Mymouse said, "but it's a secret."

"It is?"

"Yes."

"Why?"

"Because of Lord Punchkiss. The name we're talking about has a spell on it. It can even make a housequake happen."

"Why?" probed Dean.

"I don't know," Mymouse said. "Honestly. I don't."

"Then let's talk about things that don't have to be secrets. Like why you're here at the Upside Down Theatre."

Mymouse thought this over. "Kristal calls it the badness of the sadness."

Dean's look was suddenly compassionate. "What do you mean?"

"I know too much now. I have to go back. To before. I have to learn less."

"About what?"

"About everything."

Dean just looked at Mymouse for a moment. Then he said, "I see. I think. But how are you going to learn less?"

Mymouse smiled. "Almost Perfect Things."

"Now that's very interesting. What are Almost Perfect Things?"

"Oh, things I remember. Lovable things. Leona Ly can tell you better than me. She helps me remember them."

And naturally Leona Ly insisted on joining in, so I made a place for her on my left hand.

"Do you prefer to be called Miss Ly?" Dean asked her formally. "Or Ms.?"

She straightened her shoulders and I could tell she was impressed. "You may call me Leona Ly."

"Would you tell me about Almost Perfect Things?"

Leona Ly nodded her large tawny head. "Kristal would say that only perfect things count in this world. But since there are no perfect things, we must make do with Almost Perfect Things."

"Can you give me an example?" Dean asked.

The forehead of my lioness wrinkled into concentration. Then she said, "Pinpoints of fire blinking at us on a warm dark night. And towering trees bursting into flame."

"Sounds," piped in Mymouse. "Of the wind and waterfalls and birds and the laughter of little people. And the rustle of leaves made of gold."

Dean sighed. "Just like back home. In Michigan."

"And smells," said Mymouse. "Hot chocolate in the kitchen when you come in from sledding."

"How 'bout the way things taste, you guys?" Punkey asked. "Don't you think a banana is an Almost Perfect Thing?"

Dean reached over and lifted Punkey out of my backpack. "I think so, Punkey. I happen to love bananas. In fact, all these things are great. But, Mymouse, how do they help you to—"

At that moment the knock came at the Community Room door, and Mrs. Lewis looked in. "Ready?"

I said yes, and it seemed strange to be talking in my own voice again.

The door closed and Dean moved close to me for a second.

"You understand about them, don't you?" I said.

He dropped a kiss on Mymouse's head. Then he leaned over and kissed me on the lips. When he drew back his beautiful eyes were alight with tenderness.

Only I'd said it, Jessie. I'd said the most forbidden of all words—Max. And during the performance Dean seemed to be watching me much more closely than usual.

The performance itself was frightening.

Mymouse:	I think he's near—I can hear his rumbling— the Master of Disaster!
Punkey:	If he tries anything tonight, I'll chop off his head.
Kristal:	Listen, you two. I've thought it all through and I know what to do. What I hate about quakes is the way the house shakes. But it won't make a sound if we nail it all down.
Mymouse:	What do we nail down, Kristal?
Kristal:	Everything—and we've all got to do it. And when nails don't work, then we'll have to glue it.
Leona Ly:	That's a wonderful plan.
Kristal:	And if we use our heads when we want to hide, we can nail down our beds and just climb inside.
Punkey:	Now I get it. We won't have things falling all over us and it'll drive Punchkiss crazy!
Mymouse:	A great idea. Let's get to work.

113

	(All four puppets begin gluing, nailing, and tying down everything that moves in the Upside Down Theatre. Just as they finish they hear the familiar roaring sound of Lord Punchkiss, and the whole theatre begins to shake.)
Punkey:	Housequake! Housequake! Run for your life! (But this time it is curiously quiet inside and nothing moves.)
Mymouse:	Leona Ly?
Leona Ly:	Yes, Mymouse.
Mymouse:	Are you all right?
Leona Ly:	My tummy's a little shaky, but I didn't get hurt.
Mymouse:	Your idea was *fantastic*, Kristal. It really did work.
Punkey:	What about me? Doesn't anybody care how I am?
Leona Ly:	Of course, Punkey. How are you?
Punkey:	I'll have you know I'm not a bit hurt. And I wasn't even scared either.
Mymouse:	(Looking upward) We outsmarted you this time, Punchkiss. Thanks to our Kristal.
Punkey:	(Also looking up) Yeah, you Big Babbling Bossy Beast. *We* had the last laugh for a change!
Mymouse:	You know, Punchkiss must be pretty puzzled by now. Because I think he likes to feel things break and hear us scream. Only tonight that didn't happen.
Punkey:	(Laughing) I just wish I could have seen his face.
Kristal:	Oh, Punkey, no—no one ever has and no one ever will. The Master's looks can kill.

When it was over and the children were gone, I could tell Dean's mood had become even more reflective.

"I like those Almost Perfect Things," he said during our walk home. "I remember them, too."

"You do?"

"Especially the trees on fire and all. I still miss them. I haven't been in Michigan since sixth grade, but I still miss the fall."

"The fall," I repeated.

"And sledding, Carla. That, too. Winter just isn't the same out here." A pause. "So where are you from? Originally?"

"San Diego."

"I mean, when did you live somewhere besides California?"

"I never have."

Dean laughed. "Snow in San Diego, huh? And leaves turning? I only wish."

Leaves turning to gold, Jessie. Autumn. I'd never made that connection before, and it was exhilarating.

"Did you ever catch fireflies in a bottle?" he asked.

I couldn't remember.

"You haven't lived here all your life, Carla. But he's told you you have. Hasn't he?"

When Dean and I talk, there is never any question about who "he" is.

When I didn't reply, Dean asked, "What does it say on your birth certificate?"

"About what?"

"Where you were born, silly."

"I'm not sure."

"Say again?"

"I mean, I've never seen it. It was lost in a fire."

"Oh, sure."

My exasperation grew. "I have my baptismal certificate."

"What does it say?"

"San Diego."

"I figured that."

"Don't start now, Dean."

"Okay, but listen. No—I'm not going to say anything. Except—well, all right. What about pictures? Early snapshots. The background in them, I mean. I'll bet we could tell if it wasn't California."

I didn't want to say it, but I went ahead. "No pictures."

"None?"

"No. It was really hard for my dad after my mother died. I asked him once, and he said he destroyed them all—the pictures—because he couldn't bear seeing them."

"And since then?"

"What do you mean?"

"He hasn't taken any pictures since your mother died, Carla?"

"No, we're not really into that sort of thing."

"Not even on Christmas? Or birthdays?"

"I can't talk about this anymore," I said. "I have to be home."

"Oh—right," Dean said, his sarcasm powered by rage. "You'd better go for sure. And I'd better, too. Since it's some kind of capital crime for you to be with me."

I felt ashamed, and helpless to change things.

And I was afraid.

So I let him go.

Mama, it's raining, and you come in and hold me till I'm warm and rock me and sing to me. Broder comes over and tickles my feet and then you say you love me and Broder says, Do you love me, Mama? and you say, Yes, *min* Max, only then the thunder makes a big noise and I scream and squeeze you tight as I can and say, Please, Mama, don't let the nightmonster come.

Four

NOT LONG NOW, *my father.*

The sun climbs higher and it is time to make ready your bill of indictment.

According to my rules, of course.

And I should note here that in an extraordinary way, you've been consistent. Life is a game, you are so fond of saying, with no place for conventional morality. God is dead, could we but find the courage to bury Him.

Yes. Such is your credo.

But in my world, there is still evil.

And in my bill of indictment, there are to be charges; there are to be counts.

It is an age of computers, my father. And perhaps the slings and arrows of our outrageous relation to each other can be quantified. Thus somehow set to rights.

It might be fitting to construct a point scale. That should appeal to your competitive spirit. Fifty points for each time you used me sexually while I was unconscious. One hundred points for each time I was awake. One hundred and

117

fifty for my deflowering and all occasions that included that slime they call pornography. So many points for the licking up of urine and the ingestion of my own vomit. And the kicking. The beating. Certainly the choking.

Nor should we overlook such factors as age, height and weight in our calculations. Surely you deserve highest marks for incidents occurring when I was five and you were twenty-seven, when you were double my height, quadruple my body weight.

To sum up, we will adopt the policy that your point count be inversely proportional to the degree to which you gave me a sporting chance.

Yes, the points, my father. No matter how they are reckoned, they all seem to be on your side.

Perhaps your execution will earn me points, too.

A windfall to even the score.

Jessie, why is the night so long?

I'm sitting here in my rocking chair, my thoughts swarming around me without meaning or pattern, like bees. For the first time, I'm even finding it a burden to write to you.

You see, it's Friday night and I'm waiting for Dean's call. We haven't talked to each other in so long that I'm afraid.

And it's been such a peculiar day already. I haven't seen or talked to my father at all. He usually leaves a note or calls me before he finally comes home. But not today.

Also I found out that my counselor, the ever-aware Mrs. Forsythe, is still watching me. And that the staff grapevine at Jefferson High works amazingly well.

After third period today, Mrs. Forsythe called me into her office. The first thing she said was, "I heard about this morning."

I tried for a bewildered look.

She pursed her lips as if the gesture would help her contain her frustration. "You fainted during your archery class."

By now I was ready. "Just for a second though. Because I skipped breakfast."

"What did Mrs. Robles say?"

Mrs. Robles is the school nurse I saw afterwards. Her response was to take my temperature and suggest that I go home. I willed myself into a more casual and healthy-looking posture. "She didn't say anything really."

She closed her eyes for a moment as though to fortify her patience. "Your attempts to minimize this are brave, Carla, in some wrong-headed kind of way. And certainly typical. But you've got to see a doctor. How about that one treating you for anemia?"

Doctor, I thought. By all means. Perhaps one of my father's useful old contacts—his two-fisted Irish drinking buddy—Michael Cunningham, M.D.

"Carla?"

"Yes?"

"You seem distracted."

"I'm sorry, Mrs. Forsythe. I'll go to the doctor. I promise."

She seemed to relax a little. "Will you let me know what he says?"

I nodded, feeling annoyed at her interference, yet somehow warmed by it.

"Have you always been this thin?" she asked softly.

"Yes."

"Well, there is a problem that girls—mostly teenagers—can get sometimes. A losing-weight condition. People who have it just keep on losing because they think they're too heavy. Even though they might be completely emaciated."

"Not me," I said. "I know I'm thin. And I'm not trying to lose more weight."

"Yet you have. At least since school started this year. Could you just mention that to the doctor? Or has he already noticed?"

"Uh—no, not yet," I said.

She wrote down the name of the disease on a piece of paper, which was quite unnecessary because I've read about anorexia nervosa and already diagnosed that I don't have it. I reached for the paper anyway, only now Mrs. Forsythe was studying me again, and this time looking oddly furtive.

Her hand fluttered at the back of her hair, and there seemed to be more color in her face now. "I want to bring up one last thing, dear. But I don't want in any way to offend you. I'm only going to mention this on the chance it might be the problem."

And I thought: Will this never end?

"Some girls—especially these days, with changing values and all . . ." I could tell from her look that she hoped I would relieve her of the need to go on.

But I couldn't. The small office was suddenly warm, even stifling, and I was starting to feel woozy again.

"Unplanned pregnancies do happen," said Mrs. Forsythe, her tone hushed now as though she were afraid someone else might hear.

I reached out and gripped the edge of her desk. "Oh, no. No. Really, Mrs. Forsythe." I took a deep, steadying breath. "Please stop worrying about me. I'll go to the doctor. I promise."

"I'm sorry," she was saying. "I didn't mean to hurt your feelings. Only to try and cover all the possibilities."

Yes, innocent one. All the possibilities.

I tried to smile. "It's okay. I know you're trying to help. But I just happen to be the sickly looking type." I half rose. "Is it all right if I go to class now? I have a test in chemistry."

Her look of defeat touched me. "You'll let me know about the doctor?" Promising again that I would, I made my escape.

Later, Jessie, I did figure out why I fainted this morning. It's because I haven't slept in the past forty-eight hours or so and my appetite is off. I'm also starting to feel a strange tightness below my Adam's apple. A most peculiar sensation I associate with fear.

Of what? That's what I keep asking myself. The only thing I'm consciously worried about is that plan Dean mentioned in his letter. Because Dean's plans nearly always involve some kind of scheme to "liberate" me from my home. Or, as he so tactfully puts it, to deliver me up from slavery.

I have to admit there's something else, too, that I've been avoiding. About that van Dean is borrowing. Some kids refer to a van as a floating bedroom, and I know he could be planning an intimate kind of thing between us tomorrow. Especially after what I said that day at the beach about having sex with him some time.

At least it would be dark in the van, with the doors closed and all. Dean must never see my scarred body in the light, of course. Not when I'm naked. Because there is no way in the world I could explain it to him.

But I'm not afraid of Dean, if that's what you're thinking. He's the one person I have loved in twelve years. And it's such a small thing to do for him. Besides, no matter what it's like, it could never be like it is with—the other.

Dean doesn't like girls that much anyway, so maybe we could just kind of lie there in each other's arms. Sometimes I think if we could hold each other that way, we would be safe forever.

Waiting—that's all I've done since I received Dean's letter. Nothing else matters at all.

Tonight, when I hear his voice, my life will begin again.

An hour ago my father arrived home, and even as I heard him come up the stairs, I could sense the fury in his movements, in the ominous sound of his footsteps.

"Carla!"

Instantly on guard, I got to my feet. "In here, Dad."

He stopped in the doorway, breathing hard, his lips curled with malice. "Now what did you go and do?"

I sank back down into my rocking chair and made a frantic examination of conscience. "Nothing, Dad."

His face was ashen. "Does the name Forsythe ring a bell?"

Forsythe, I thought. Mrs. Forsythe?

"I'm waiting, Carla. And don't you dare lie to me."

"She's my counselor at school."

"I know she's your fucking counselor. I found that out today."

I froze. "You did?"

"You did?" he mimicked. "What did you expect, the way you've been spilling your guts to her?"

Keep calm, I told myself. Hold steady. "No, Dad. She questioned me, but I haven't told her anything. Nothing at all."

He made a sudden movement toward me, then caught himself. "Liar! She called me at the office. Said you've got problems and you have to see a doctor. So what the hell is that?"

I tried to still the tremor in my throat. "That's all *her* idea, Dad. She watches me. Thinks I look sick, tired, whatever. But that's *all*."

The lines in his forehead deepened. "You expect me

122

to buy that?" But I could see belief germinating in him now.

"It's true, Dad. I swear. She called me in because I fainted during archery. And she's all worried about me, you know? So I just told her I'm anemic and the doctor's giving me pills for it."

The taut line of my father's massive shoulders loosened. "Is that the truth?"

"Yeah, Dad. She's just real curious."

Letting out a long breath, he began massaging his temples. "So how come you fainted anyway?"

"Not enough sleep I guess. And I didn't eat breakfast this morning."

He studied me for a moment. "Have you been taking those iron pills I got you?"

"Sure, Dad."

"Better double up on 'em."

"Okay."

He looked tired himself, his bearlike hands hanging loosely now at his sides. "Christ, I had a bad day."

"Me, too."

His blue eyes grew hard. "What the hell would you know about a bad day, kid?" He drew the back of his hand slowly across his forehead. "Most people in my business are really hurting right now. And everybody's got to put up with things they wouldn't ever have put up with before. Like all the ass you have to kiss to make one lousy sale. And sometimes even that doesn't work. Like Ralston tonight—my so-called client. The one I thought I had that beach deal with, that big-money deal. Having second thoughts, he says. Second fucking thoughts. And he has the nerve to throw in that he doesn't like high-pressure salesmen. Didn't say it about me directly, of course, but he got his point across all right. If that deals falls through it'll really set us back."

He didn't say anything more for a long moment, and then a look of amazement passed over his face. "I worked twelve hours today. No wonder I'm draggin'. If my old man had any idea how tough this business is. . . . Makes the cops look like a picnic. Especially in places like Longfield. Those guys just sit around on their duffs ninety percent of the time. On Saturday night they cruise Main Street and maybe roust a drunk or two. Or they'll get a call on some weenie waver. But nothing really happens for a year. Don't believe all that shoot 'em up stuff you see on tv, kid. Those guys couldn't hustle a real living if their lives depended on it."

A new word was hanging in the air. New and yet oddly evocative . . . Longfield.

My father rubbed his eyes. "Christ, that Forsythe woman annoyed the hell out of me. Sounded just like that caseworker when you were younger. The one nosy Velma sent over that time. The worker asked me all those crazy questions, like what we did together and if I read stories to you and that. Even had the gall to ask me if you had any toys. As if toys were going to make it up to you for losing your mother. Sure, you were lonely. Sure, you didn't smile. What'd they expect? Your mother dead and me sweating my guts out to make us a living." My father was shaking his head incredulously. "She practically insisted you go see some shrink. And it was Velma Saunders that sent her, even though she denied it. 'Why doesn't Carla smile?' Velma'd always say. 'Why's she so quiet?' "

> Kristal: The sadness face will have to go.
> If you don't smile the world will know.
> The badness here must never show.

". . . asked a slew of questions about your mother, too. Imagine. So I finally told her to go fuck herself. Politely,

124

of course. Can't get those do-gooders upset or they never let you alone. But I told her to just leave your mother out of it. Mental problems can't be passed on."

Those last words enthralled me.

He sighed. "Sure, so she had a few problems now and then. But nothing that could affect you. All that heredity stuff is just plain bull."

I kept my voice serenely controlled. "My mother had mental problems?"

"Hey, look, those doctors get in on it and they could make you believe anything, Carla. I mean—depression. Do you know how many people are depressed in this world? So she was depressed sometimes. So what?"

My heart raced and a question erupted in my head: did you treat her the way you treat me?

Of course, you did. How stupid of me not to think of it before. How selfish and blind can I be?

And for the first time I thought about the fact that my parents had a life together, however brief, before I was born.

And my mother was depressed. Just like me.

Unsettling thoughts, Jessie. Dangerously unsettling.

"Those shrinks," Dad went on. "Goddamned meddlers. Go rummaging around in other people's heads like they had a right to. So I just came out and told her. You and me have something going she could never understand. Because when it came down to the final choice, I chose you. Gave up everything I had to do it."

Mystified and afraid, I didn't speak.

Then he said with unexpected tenderness, "C'mere, girl." When I drew near, he put his arm around me. "Don't we now?"

"What?"

"Have something really special?"

I tried to smile. "Sure, Dad."

He kissed my cheek. "You're mine, baby. Flesh of my flesh. Bone of my bone." I tried not to stiffen when he held me closer. "My loyal little girl."

Then he licked his lips and looked around as though to make sure we were alone. When he spoke again, his tone was noticeably sharper: "I'm counting on you. Watch that bitch at school. You don't know what kind of trouble she could cause. I want her out of our business for good. If it'll shut her up, I can get Mike Cunningham to write her some kind of statement about your health."

"I can handle it," I said. "Don't worry."

He gave me a wan smile. "Yeah, good. 'Cause they're all jackals out there, Carla. Eat you alive if they get the chance. And just remember, nobody'll ever take care of you like your own dad."

His physical closeness was suddenly so oppressive I thought I couldn't bear it.

But all at once he was pulling away again. "Jesus—what a day! Do I need a drink."

And then he was gone.

About those things he said, Jessie. Those very disturbing things. Part of me does want to understand about them and to know more. But another part, the miserable groveling coward that lives inside me, doesn't.

And the coward wins, I'm afraid. I will ask no more questions. Engulfed as I am in secrets, I choose not to know what lies behind the well-closed doors.

I will concentrate on what is good in my life.

I will think only of Dean.

How did I come to indulge myself in this feast of pain?

When I believed that tonight there would be a pardon. Or at least a reprieve.

Illusion, Jessie. Delusion. Hallucination and confusion.

I am dreaming of who I am. Am I Carla? Am I Jean? Or Carla Jean? Yes. At once the daughter and the wife.

She lives within me and I in her. My mother. Female parent. Origin or source. Spun-gold hair and gentle hands. Soft accented speech.

Mama.

No, you fool—an illusion. A false idea the truth may penetrate at last.

Or delusion. A false idea that cannot be toppled by anything.

Which, Mama? Which are you?

Father. Male parent. Origin or source. From his seed came I and then the picture went awry.

I, created from his seed, ingest it now to fill his need.

Ingest. Incest. *Incestus*. Yes—unendingly impure, in order to endure.

Jessie. You're concerned for my sanity. Alas, you are too late. It is unavailable for questioning.

And please just answer me something—tell me why the big words, the ones formed so ponderously, are so simple to grasp? But show me a word of one syllable or two— *trust, rape, ruin, love*—and I will show you an invention to torture and paralyze the mind. I will show you the incomprehensible.

A word like *father*. My father. Carl Jay Hughes. Defined as my food, my shelter, my clothing. And a face I have looked into more than all other faces combined, those guiltless blue eyes, the hypnotic smiles, the voice whose tones I took in like mother's milk, the figure so utterly familiar in its shape and movements, the man who tells me I am his and there is nothing in the world but us two.

Yet when I awaken on the floor beside my bed, his bare feet are next to my face and he is ordering me into his bed.

I follow him, meekly obedient, lie down for him just as I'm told. And I think: I am seventeen and nothing has changed.

It is one of those nights when alcohol seems to revive him. He pulls off loose-fitting boxer shorts, exposing his flaccid buttocks and then, as he turns around, the loathesome thing that hangs between his legs.

As yet untouched, I already feel unclean. And I think: How can I do it? Be with my love tomorrow? After this night buried alive in my father's bed?

He is with me now, moving heavily against me, his rank breath tainting my face. I say, "Please," but without hope.

He raises himself on one elbow and flexes his arm like a weapon, his fist and the long muscles of his forearm inches from my eyes. "No backtalk, Jeannie. I know damn well what you want."

My mother's name. Always proof that violence is in him.

I whimper foolishly.

He thrusts his groin against my leg. "It'll still be the same for us, Jeannie. Forget those lies my old man told your father. I was never with her. That dumb slut. The boy isn't mine. It's all lies."

"Dad—no."

"Shut your mouth!" He twists one of my breasts savagely. I gasp. But he is distracted by his disappointment. "Christ, Jeannie, what the hell happened to your tits? They're nothing anymore." He pushes me away from him like an unwanted toy.

And I think to myself: No. I am moved at last to rebellion.

No more.

And I find it's there already—the numbness I crave. There for me now. The sweet anesthesia. And it says: Go ahead. Let it happen. Bring it on. Sweet numbing peace.

Far away, I hear the long-awaited signal from Dean, two rings of the telephone, but still I feel nothing.

My father is ranging above me and I can see that he isn't aroused, that all of this is rage. He motions what he wants me to do for him, snarling as if to say: you are as detestable as you are useful.

I shake my head monotonously back and forth, back and forth on the pillow. He pulls me up by the shoulders; I remain limp as a rag doll between his hands. Stay with me, sweet numbness. Don't desert me now.

He slaps me hard across the face, then once or twice more. I can feel the force of these blows, but not the pain. For I am looking down on us now, on the two of us, the grotesque couple locked together on the big bed.

"Slut," he says. "You won't say no to me."

My head moves back and forth with suicidal ease.

And all at once, in an ominously familiar movement, my father eases one of his legs down to the floor for leverage and straddles my body, his big hands encircling my throat. In the vise of his grasp, my head becomes a balloon squeezed at the neck, my forehead and temples tight with swelling blood. My mouth locks downward on both sides and I can feel the protrusion of my own blinking eyes, the merciless crushing of my chest. In clownlike spasms my drawn-up legs thrash vainly behind my father's back. His lips are taut, his teeth bared, the cords of his neck engorged with effort, and his labored rasp mingles with the sounds of my choking. The roaring comes in my ears; my vision shrinks and falters. I command my arms to rise and help me; my fingers pull feebly at his rocklike thumbs. And I try to move the mouth in my frozen face.

But it's too late. Pinpoints of light herald my approaching death. Into my chest comes the inevitable explosion of terror.

I can't scream.

* * *

129

A field.

Farmland stretching long and lonely into an endless horizon. The ground naked. The trees black with rain. Far down from me in the field is a figure twisting darkly in the wind.

A woman.

I want to run to her. Frigid rain falls on me and I pull. But it's no use. I'm strangling in an iron collar. Small as a kitten, on a leash held fast by a giant's hand. A leash in the enormous fingers of the nightmonster. I strain more and can't breathe, my neck and throat seared with pain. But I keep on because I'm scared she will move away from me. And vanish.

The collar binds me, but we are moving forward at last and I can see it more clearly. See that it isn't a woman at all. It's a stick; on the stick is an old dress stuffed with straw. It's a scarecrow flapping in the chill rainy wind.

I look up at the nightmonster. His mouth is opened wide and he is laughing.

Mama, it's real hot today. I put on my sun dress by myself only I can't reach in the back so Daddy does it. Then he braids my hair and talks softlike and calls me his Goldilocks. After that he puts the end of my braid in his mouth and laughs and his mouth is big and he says, I can eat you up, Goldilocks, I can eat you *all* up. His teeth are yellow and in the back they have silver and I see his dark red tongue. I ask him, When can we go, Daddy? He bounces up and says, Right now—I promised you and we will. Then we get in the car and drive for a long way and after a while I can smell that smell where the wind and the sand are together and I think, Now I'm near my other house. Near you, Mama, and my Broder. I say out loud,

Where's my Mama? And Daddy puts his fist down hard on the wheel. She's dead. How many times do I have to tell you, Carla? Dead!

Only I know you're alive, Mama. I said good-bye to you before I left that time with my Daddy. I cry anyway 'cause he scares me and I put my hand over my mouth and say inside me, Don't talk, and then we come to the place where the Cyclone Racer is. Daddy is happy again. He holds my hand and we walk into the big park and I know you will be there, Mama, waiting to surprise me. Only they fixed everything a different way and the trees are all gone and I don't see you. I only see cotton candy and that makes me hungry. I ask Daddy for some, but he says, Not till later, I don't want you getting sick. Daddy walks so fast I get tired right away, and we see a lady as big as a whole house and a man who is turning into a stone. He doesn't move, but I am scared of him anyway.

I can't wait for the roller coaster, Mama, 'cause I know you'll be waiting there, but when we come to it, it isn't the Cyclone Racer anymore, not the one with you and Broder. This one is the biggest I ever saw and the man's hat is blue and he says to my Daddy, She's too small, and my Daddy says, She's been on here before and she isn't afraid of anything. But the man says, It's against the rules, and Daddy makes a face and shakes his finger and says, Then break the stupid rule. So the other man doesn't look at us anymore and he just says, Oh, go ahead then, and we get in the car. This one is painted blue and Daddy says, That bastard sure had a nerve. I just feel scared, Mama, 'cause I don't see you yet. Daddy holds me real tight and the iron thing comes down on us so we won't fall out. And I think, Where is Broder? I like to ride with him best of all. Daddy presses too hard and he squashes me. Then we start to move and some people are saying Oh-h-h and we are going up. It's far to go up, a long, long way, and Daddy holds me and we get up real high and then my breath stops and we're flying down and deeper down fast enough to die.

My eyes are shut and I'm so scared I can't scream and I want to get off now, but we are going up again and I just keep my eyes closed and want it to be over. And it happens more and after a long time it's getting slow and then it stops. When we get out Daddy has to help me and my arm is sore and so is my knee, but I don't care. I just want to find you, Mama, right now. Daddy's smiling and breathing real hard and he says, It's the best coaster in the world. But I don't see you, Mama, and I feel bad inside and I say, I was never on this one before, Daddy. It's for big people. Daddy squeezes my hand and he says, Yes, you were. It's a different ocean, I say, not the one where Broder is and Daddy tells me, Shut up. This is the exact same one, Carla. You never remember things right. I say, Okay, Daddy, even though I know. You listen to *me*, Daddy says real fast. You believe what *I* say. Yes, Daddy.

Then I see the cotton candy again and ask for some, and he says, Just like a female—always wanting something. We stop at the cotton candy and I watch the lady catch it on the white paper and then my strap comes undone and Daddy fixes it and he buys me some cotton candy. So we start walking again till I see a lady with golden hair just like yours, Mama, and I think it's you. Come on, Daddy says, and he pulls me. But I say, No, wait, there's my Mama! Only when the lady looks at me, she isn't you, Mama. She's some other lady, and Daddy takes the cotton candy away from me and throws it in the trash can. You don't love me, he says, and his face is all red and mad. You love her more than anybody and she's dead.

He grabs my hand again and walks us real fast so I have to run to keep up. Then we're at the car and he puts the key in the door and tells me to get in the back. And when he gets in next to me he pushes me down on the seat and my head is under the place where you can put your arm and his eyes look funny. He pulls my leg up on his knees. His face is different now and his eyes don't look at me and he puts his hand under my dress. He feels my tummy and there is noise in my ears. He puts his other hand over my mouth and my tummy hurts so much I'm wiggling. Then he says, Don't move or I'll do it more. He keeps his hand over my mouth and I can't breathe every time and I try not to move but it's too hard. Daddy takes his hand off my tummy and undoes his belt. I'm lying still now 'cause I can breathe more when I stay still.

Daddy moves a little and he looks at my legs and he puts his finger inside my panties. Then the loggie comes up on his leg and he's holding it and breathing fast and then he pulls off my panties and says, This is all you're good for anyway. His hand gets harder on my mouth and I can't breathe and then I can and his other hand is on my legs. He's making fast noises and I feel something in the place where I go pinka and it burns me and my eyes get black inside.

When I wake up Daddy is looking at me. It was only my finger, he says. You're too goddamned small for anything else. Then he puts his hand on my head and touches my hair real soft the way you do, Mama. I want something to take the burning away. I start crying. I need to go to the bathroom, Daddy. Not if you cry. It hurts too much. I'll drive you home and you can go there. No, please, Daddy, I can't wait. Stop crying then. He lifts up my dress again and his hands are shaking and he looks at me, you're all right. Listen to your Daddy. You're just fine. A little sore, that's all.

He opens the car door, but when I try to walk, I can't. So even though I'm big, Daddy carries me. We stop in front of the bathroom and Daddy looks around and says, Nobody's here so I'll take you in. But I know Daddy can't go in where girls go. When we get inside a lady is in front of the mirror. You'd better go outside, she tells Daddy. I'll see she's all right. So he puts me down and goes away.

The lady takes me to the toilet and I try to go but it hurts too much. And I try not to cry but then I do and she says, What's wrong, sweetie? And I say, It hurts where I go pinka. I go a little and then I scream. When I pull my panties up the lady looks in the toilet. She smiles at me then and says, Don't worry, honey, you'll be okay. She talks nice like you, Mama, and she says, What's your name? I say, Carla. Your whole name, honey? And I say, Carla Inger Hughes. And then she says, How old are you? And I say Six, only then I remember Daddy said that's a mistake, and I'm really five. So I say Five. And then she puts her face right down by mine and says, Who's that man outside? And I say, My Daddy. Oh, she says, and then she smiles again. That's good. She takes me to Daddy and says, Your little girl is hurt. She needs to go to the doctor. He picks me up in his arms and I can feel him shaking all over. She fell down a minute ago, he says. I wondered if she hurt herself. His hand is squeezing my leg underneath my dress. I'll get her right home. Better go to the doctor, the lady says. There was a little red in the toilet. And Daddy says real nice, I will.

He carries me away from there sort of fast but not running, and the way he is holding me makes it hurt more. When we get to the car he puts me down but he holds onto my arm and gets the key out with his other hand and opens the door. He puts me in the back seat again and he gets in the front and we start driving and his voice is yelling, You little bitch! You almost got me in trouble! The car seat is bumping me and the hurt between

134

my legs is bad and I hold myself there and I rock myself on the seat the way you rock me, Mama. And I know how bad I am. I almost got my daddy in trouble. He says, You listening, Carla? Yes. Say yes, *Daddy!* And I say, Yes, Daddy. Don't you ever pull anything like that on me again. If you do, I'll drive you out to the desert and leave you there. All alone. To die.

Then Daddy says, What happened is you fell down, hear me? If I say it happened that way, it did. You *listen* to me, get it? Only me. And I promise Daddy I'll never get him in trouble again. But he's still mad at me. And I didn't even see you today, Mama. I thought you would be there by the Cyclone Racer, but you never came.

I hate everything, Mama, if I don't have you.

I awaken in my room. Lying like a princess on top of my canopy bed. My throat and lungs on fire.

My father is standing near the foot of the bed. He moves closer, cautiously, as though he doesn't want to frighten me. My hand gropes for the bottle of aspirin I keep on my nightstand. He reaches over and takes it up himself. He says, in the reverent tone he sometimes uses afterwards, "I'll get some water."

I can hear him in the bathroom and I feel reassured by his mood, but the flame in my chest is trying to consume me.

He brings me a cup and the tablets, and I make myself sit up to take them, ordering the ruthless throb of pain to subside, choking as the pills go down.

A mute and faithful servant, my father waits for me, takes back the cup and sets it on my nightstand.

I lie down again and the light from the hall settles eerily on his face.

After a long time, he says, "There's something you have

to realize, Carla. About us, I mean." He speaks slowly, measuring the words out as if I were a child. "I don't think you get it yet—what you are and what I am. And what I'm trying to build for the two of us. You're a female, that's first. And you have to learn to be a real woman. See? I've got what you're wanting right here, and that's nature. That's good. And I know a woman likes to be forced sometimes, too—I realize that. So she fights and it's better for her at the end. Okay. Only sometimes you just fight me too much, Carla, and I have to stop you." He stopped for a moment. "But I'm a strong man, and maybe something bad could happen. Something that could never be put right."

For a minute there is silence in my room. He has moved away from the light now and I hear him sigh. "There's something else, too, baby. It's about how skinny you are now—it's terrible. A man doesn't want his girl too thin like that. Looks like I'm not feeding you or something. And it just isn't—I don't want you as much when you're this way. I'm not trying to hurt your feelings, but it's ugly, you know? Not the way it used to be for us, the past years. Then it was fine. Even when you were real young, the way you'd want me to do things to you all the time. The way you'd climb up in my lap and rub against me with that sweet little bottom. Or crawl into bed with me in your nightie. I'd get excited right away. You've always had this thing about you, this sex thing I mean. Some girls are like that, made for love. And it's fine— don't get me wrong. A real man wants that. But you have to let me lead the way. You have to know that you belong to a man. That's the first thing you have to learn. And more than anything I need for you to believe in me. It's because of you I keep going in this life. So you have to take care of yourself more. Put some weight on. And let your hair grow out, too. I'll make it worth your while, baby. When we get our house at the ocean, you can stay home all the time if you want. Read and just do the things you like to do. As long as you remember that what's important is us. Only us."

I wait till I am sure he is finished speaking and then make this ugly grunting noise to get his attention. He looks at me, then sits down beside me on the bed. I swallow and the pain overtakes me for a minute and then I make myself say, "You hurt me."

He raises his hand to cover his ears, as though to shut out the already-spoken words. "No. I don't do that. No. You've got some pain right now, Carla. It's just the pain talking." His body relaxes unexpectedly. He smiles at me and pats my hand. "Don't worry. That wasn't aspirin I gave you before. It was a couple of good strong pain pills. They'll help you sleep."

What he says doesn't matter; I have already surrendered. And after a time the succoring warmth of the medication does begin to enfold me, to erode the wicked edge of this pain. . . .

Again, I awaken, scarcely aware I have been dozing.

He is still with me, sitting on the edge of my bed. Our eyes meet, but between my father and me there is a great stillness.

He is waiting for the last of it.

Because this is our dance, Jessie: classic, stylized, preordained. We await only the final steps—one my father's, one mine.

Finally his comes: "Carly, are you all right?"

And that is the question I've been waiting for, those words, suffused as they always are with fear and love.

Now I can feel his watchful tension and it is his turn to wait.

I have him. For just this one instant he is waiting for me, his vulnerability a quivering thread between us. And it is this very thread that disarms me, dissolving my rage, making trivial my despair.

Freely, shamelessly, I thrust back to him my one moment of power. And verify his ownership, underscore his absolute right. All with a single monstrous falsehood conveyed by nothing more than a subtle inclination of my head.

Yes, I nod to him in reply, I am all right. And when I do this, I release in both of us a kind of tranquility. A shared resolution.

The medication wraps tender arms around me.

Jessie, I can close my eyes. You will think me mad, of course, but now it is good.

At the last it is always good. When the nightmonster has gone and there is only my father and me.

Five

I AM VIGILANT, *my father.*

Innocent sleep, that "balm of hurt minds" Macbeth speaks of, is not possible for us.

We murder sleep.

Besides, the day is full upon us now and the time of your trial nearly at hand.

I grapple with the final points of your indictment. I turn from the rape of a body to the devastation of a mind.

And I wonder: Am I going to kill you because you steeped my life in humiliation, built your frail confidence on the wreckage of mine?

Or will I do it because you confounded me with lies about all that matters? Made my reality as unstable and treacherous as quicksand?

Yes, the latter. For a decade of humiliation can at least be examined openly along the way. But a decade of deception uncoils in secret, patient as a viper that silently readies itself for the mortal sting.

Only now it is I who am a viper.

Made so by your betrayal, my father. My Machiavelli. You. To whom this mastery of lies must seem a hallmark of greatness. My father, the king. The king who would be prince. Who banishes truth—so troublesome, so untidy— who disdains the edicts of time and takes his own daughter to wife.

Enough. I ask myself now, is your indictment complete? But no—for we must not forget the continual proximity of death, or the manner in which this prospect suffocates the human spirit.

We must not forget the witness of death itself.

You will open your mouth to dispute me—insist that it is I who have always brought death—but this time your words are foredoomed.

Because I know everything. The well-closed doors stand open now, and with a shuddering sensitivity, I confront the truth.

It turns out that you are the foolish one after all, my father. Since you did not anticipate this day yourself. Did not predict that once I was stripped of everything, I would have nothing left to lose.

So there is justice here at last, as my forefingers caress the trigger of your gun.

Not that you taught me how to shoot—the most commonplace of skills, after all—but that you taught me how to kill.

I am half-awake on this raw dark Saturday morning, and I ask myself: Where do these memories come from? Farmland extending forever? Acres of forest dense with black-trunked trees? Haunting scarecrows?

Do images intrude from another lifetime? Or am I at last unbalanced and unhinged?

I am aroused by the ringing of the telephone. I sit up and try to peer through the oppressive haze in my head. In the spaces between the rings, I detect that the house is promisingly quiet. I go to the phone in my father's bedroom.

It's Dean. As he talks to me, his voice eager and remote, I try to look away from my father's ravaged bed. My throat is so swollen I can't swallow, and Dean says it sounds like I have laryngitis. We agree to meet at the library at three and say good-bye.

For a moment I stand there in his room, naked and still trying to shake the morning cobwebs out of my brain. Then I sit down for a moment in his big bedroom chair by the window. I picture his body prone amid the bedclothes, all in a tangle from last night's confusion. I have never sat in this chair before. It's back swells thronelike behind me, and for a moment, I am heady with his power.

In this chair, I, too, could rule. Judge. Pass sentence. It is good, this chair. It is magic.

I am obsessed by this magic chair: whosoever sitteth here shall be safe from all harm.

I shiver. Then I feel a sudden urge to look into the full-length mirror on his closet door.

To see *her*—the slut. The murderous black-hearted whore.

I go to the mirror and this is how I look: each of my ribs stands out individually now, my small brown nipples looking startled by the disappearance of my meager breasts. And there is a curious space between my thighs reminiscent of a wishbone. "I can't scream" is healed, but still faintly visible on my left thigh and everywhere on my body I see the random scarring. As for my scrawny neck, it bears the unmistakable fingerprints of my father. In a story, these would be called angry red marks. As it turns out, such a description is not only appropriate in my case but symbolic. I am thinner than I was when Dean last saw me. My jaw has the droll angular lines of a nut-cracker. My body resembles a photograph from Auschwitz. For the first time I acknowledge that Dean could be revolted as well as bewildered by this sight.

My father's bathrobe hangs from a hook on the door to my right. I take a moment to spit on it. Then I look back at my reflection, soothed by the sight of my own tran-scendent ugliness. I am no longer nondescript, Jessie; I have dramatic impact now.

And imagine: last night this raddled excuse for a hu-man being was out cold as a corpse.

Yet still he wanted to do it.

The putrescent odor that emanates from me at this mo-ment tells me that he did.

A smell that cannot be extinguished. My body as hope-less of cleansing as Lady Macbeth's blood-drenched hands.

And the odor is not his alone any longer, but his and mine.

An odor suggestive of all that rots.

I am lying on the floor again in my room, breathing in the silence of this house. And I know you're still there, Jessie, waiting so patiently for your answer.

All you want to know is why.

But what if I tell you that's what *I* want to know?

Yes.

Because it should be easy for you.

You could sift through all those satisfying hothouse insights of yours. Call on that razor-sharp understanding of high school women and men.

And tell *me* why.

No—please don't take offense. I am testy. I am cranky.

I hone a bitter edge to everything. Even now as I prepare myself to meet my love.

In the shower I enjoyed the burning of my skin. Though I will never be clean, the scalding water made me feel less filthy. When the steam entered my aching lungs, I knew the pain would be there a long time. But the agonizing of my body purged my soul, Jessie. So I feel I've earned the right to this afternoon.

Paid the price, you might say.

In advance.

I am dressed now, but the "angry red marks" snake their way revealingly up toward my chin. I take off my brown turtleneck sweater and blend makeup carefully into my neck.

My father is even more skillful at such things. When I was little, he would put the makeup on me himself. Rub it well into my skin, blend and blot it artfully so nothing would rub off onto my clothing.

My father is a master of concealment, Jessie, and so am I.

It is necessary. The outside world, though frequently lacking in compassion, is unremittingly curious.

Alas, my Dean.

For now I am looking at the final result of my efforts this morning: me, in my bulky brown sweater and too-loose jeans.

Yes, poor Dean. Even now as he sallies forth earnest as a bridegroom in his van. Probably seeking our first sexual encounter.

The one I tendered so recklessly at the beach long ago.

The offer I am bound to take back, since the skeletal ruin of my body is unfit for love. Hideously. And since it tells too many tales. He must never see me unclothed. For his own sake, I must withdraw.

But, Jessie, I love him even more for just this reason, that though Dean may not comprehend or agree with my wishes, he will respect them.

And that in him there is nothing of the brute.

No. There will be no force.

Nor hint of force.

Jessie? It's me again. Your Carla-Carlek.

Do I seem different now?

Of course I do. I'm high.

And you're incredulous. Because I said I don't do drugs, said I was scared of them, and you believed me. Drugs and booze and ghosties and goblins and things that go bump in the night.

Stay alert—stay alive.

Only a little while ago I discovered that Dad left his bottle of pain pills on my bathroom sink last night. Forgot all about them, I reckon. And my throat was still smarting like crazy, so I took another one. Pill, that is. Oh, Demerol, my Demerol, our fearful trip is done. Ah, yes. A new trip now, Jessie. The softest, most ethereal of journeys.

So my throat hardly hurts anymore, and I feel all dizzy and warm and wanting to be with my love.

But it's much too early to leave yet; I have at least another hour. So I'm sitting here in the solitude of my room. And I am all-powerful now. . . .

My dearest Jessie. See how my benumbed fingers carry on? Writing to you?

Exquisite one—how do I love thee? Let me count the ways. Elizabeth Barrett Browning. A strong woman like you, Jessie. Much stronger than Emily and I. Elizabeth escaped him. She came away with her Robert.

A woman with a wonderful name. So elegant. Even stately.

144

While yours, my Jessica Silva, is all music. A shimmering skein of sound as exultant as a harp.

Sweet Jessie, how I do love thee.

And all the more because I will never see you or speak to you or touch you. All the more because you're my own lovely invention. No, I do not resent that you have become a figment of the vulnerable core of my imagination. Your unreality is, after all, your finest attribute. It enables me to bring to you the afflictions of my vile heart.

To tell you everything.

Like now.

And you already know about my farewell-party package. The stash I keep in Mymouse's intelligent gray head.

So you see, I don't usually take drugs at all—I just hoard them. And I know by heart exactly what I have: eight Percodans... eleven Seconals... fifteen codeines... twenty-one Demerols (not counting the discreet one or two more I will remove from my father's bottle today.)

Impressive, isn't it? The way I reeled off those numbers. Only I'm not sure I didn't do a little transposing along the way—say, eleven Percodans and eight Seconals... three golden rings, two turtle doves, and a par-tri-idge in a pear tree.

All courtesy of Michael Cunningham, M.D.

Yes, Demerol. That beloved among potions. That crown jewel in my treasure trove for slumber.

Soon I will have a foolproof arsenal for making sleep Not the sleep of the innocent. Or the pure of heart. But sleep.

Deep and everlasting.

I am distraught, Jessie. I am beside myself.
No—this must begin at the beginning.

With my walk to the library. Which was quite painless in my state of drugged elevation. I was no longer nervous about seeing Dean or even cautious—only eager. I floated mindlessly above the struggles of the common herd.

Nor did I heed the overcast sky or the curious pearl-gray clouds so suggestive of evil humors. Because I didn't understand them then, Jessie. I was warm with love and the remembered scent of the ocean and the fragile pressure of his body and his mind.

Safe inside my own euphoria, I saw Dean waiting in the foyer of the library. I drifted confidently toward him, misreading the intensity in his big dark eyes. Thinking it was his emotion over seeing me—and his love.

That it was caused by horror didn't occur to me at all.

He was wearing his good slacks and a dark green corduroy shirt I'd never seen before, and somehow he looked older. He held me at arm's length, but I didn't interpret this correctly either, or his startled look and the softly incredulous shaking of his head. "Carla—hi," he said, only it sounded like a question.

I embraced him boldly.

He drew back and tugged at my hand. "Let's go. The van is parked about a block away."

On the walk I perceived the unusual stiffness of his shoulders and the joylessness of his tone, but even they didn't affect my sense of well-being.

Behind a building, at the rear of an empty parking area, was the van. It was cream-colored, with dark brown curtains drawn at the windows. Dean unlocked the door and pulled it expertly aside, motioning me in. Entering the dark cavern, I sat down on an invitingly thick piece of carpeting as Dean switched on a lamp in the corner. Then he pulled the door closed and sat down beside me. I was engrossed by the cordless lamp, which illuminated the space as gently as a candle.

146

"How did you do that?" I asked, giggling.

"It works on a battery." He was close to me, but we weren't touching.

I leaned back against him. "That's really clever," I said, all at once feeling secure and happily tired.

I don't know how long the silence was that followed. Only that when Dean broke it, his mood finally came through to me. "Carla, what's going on?"

Alerted by the strained way he spoke my name, I said, "I'm glad to be with you. Aren't you glad?"

"I want to know what's going on." He pulled away abruptly and my head lolled into the empty space he left.

"Like what you're on, for instance."

And I could feel myself starting to come down from my high. Just like that. I was annoyed by Dean's attitude and inordinately offended. "Just a pill. A pain pill."

Caring softened his tone now. "What for?"

"My—throat." A dim consciousness of dangerous ground. "It's sore."

"A pain pill for a sore throat? That doesn't make sense."

"Why not?"

Something about the lamplight on his face brought back the earnest, boyish look I'd seen so many times before. "What you need is an antibiotic. And whatever you took had to be a strong devil to get you like this."

And there he was again, practicing medicine without a license. "Like what?" I asked.

"Spacey, Carla. Real spacey. What was it anyway?"

"I don't know."

"Well, where'd you get it from then? Not from a doctor."

"Yeah. The doctor. Before. A long time ago."

"I sure can tell you've been sick all right. It's more than obvious."

Canny now, I looked at him. "What do you mean?"

"The weight you've lost—I almost didn't recognize you. I think I could have passed you by on the street."

I giggled again. "Maybe I should have worn a red carnation."

"Hey, don't be smart, okay. I don't think I can handle that right now." He moved over and slipped his arm around my waist. It took a moment of trial-and-error before we both got comfortable against the side of the van. "So I want to know what happened. Was it flu?"

I nodded gratefully, my head peaceful and safe on his shoulder now. "Yeah. I was down with it for ten days."

"You poor baby. Why didn't you tell me?"

"By the time we talked again, it was all over."

"Except for the throat," he corrected. My alert Dean.

"Right," I said.

He kissed my cheek, and then I turned my face so we could kiss each other on the lips. I like that about him so much, that we can take our time together. Go slow. And kissing him is good. Clean and comforting. It makes me forget.

"I wish you weren't high right now," he murmured into my neck.

"I'm not," I said half truthfully. "Only a little anyway. You wrecked it."

We held each other for a little while, and I could tell he wanted us to lie down, but I was afraid of that and where it might lead and pretended not to understand. Just wanting to sit there with him the way we were, just wanting to hold on to him as long as I could.

But the Demerol was wearing off now and my throat began its monotonous throb again and I suddenly felt defeated and spent.

"I've got something for you," he said lazily. "For someone who's seventeen now."

No, I wanted to say, lost in my guilt. I don't deserve it. I'm embarrassed. Please don't.

But I said nothing.

Then I saw the little white box in his hand. "Open it," he said proudly.

And in the box was a silver chain. I lifted it out and on it found a little silver strawberry glistening in the lamplight. It is flat with shiny leaves etched right around the stem and little holes in the berry itself that make it look real.

It is inexpressibly beautiful.

"I know how you like strawberries," he said, smiling.

It was hard to look at him, or even to say thank you. The tears that rose in my throat left me mute.

"Want to try it on?" he asked, understanding my silence.

Still holding up the necklace with one hand, I touched the bulky neck of my old brown sweater and remembered what lay underneath. "Not right now," I said, turning to him. "But it's wonderful."

He chuckled. "No. It's only silver. Maybe an *Almost Perfect Thing*."

"The design is so unique," I said. I put my arms around him, holding the necklace tight in my hand. Then, inexplicably and to my extreme chagrin, I was crying.

Dean's right hand was patting my back in a soothing rhythmic way, a practice of his that always makes me ache with love. "I wish we could drive away right now, Carla, and not look back."

I nodded against his shoulder, humiliated by the wetness I was leaving on his shirt.

"Some day," he said. "And sooner than you think." He handed me a folded white cloth.

The novelty of this gesture arrested my tears. "What's this?" I asked.

"A handkerchief."

"What? You have a handkerchief?"

He looked sheepish. "My Mom always made me carry one when I was younger. I still do."

"But I thought only guys in books had handkerchiefs. And you want me to wipe my eyes on it? Blow my nose even?"

"Unless you'd rather drip."

Then we were both laughing, the way we used to do. Only it did seem like a desecration for me to use the soft clean cloth that way. A real actual handkerchief. Oh, my debonair one. My Dean.

"You were born in the wrong century," I told him.

"I know," he said. "But don't be afraid to use it, Carla. That's what it's for."

I dabbed at my face with the handkerchief, then sat holding the soggy thing, unwilling to give it back to him.

"Let me wash it at home and then I'll give it back," I said. But I'll wash it separately, I thought, not with the regular laundry. Not with *his* things.

Dean was grinning at me now. "Look, do you want it? To keep, I mean?"

I studied the crumpled ball. And I thought: How good it is to be with him, to love him like this. "All right, Dean, but let's make it a real romantic thing then. I'll embroider some strawberries on it and give it back to you. Just like in *Othello*."

You'll have to fill me in," he said. "Our class read *Julius Caesar*."

I shoved his handkerchief into my pocket. "Well— Othello gives his wife this handkerchief embroidered with strawberries. It was one his father had given his mother years before. So to Othello, of course, it is a treasure. He gives it to Desdemona when they're first married—as a pledge of his love."

Dean's eyes were smiling. "That means you're Othello then. And I'm Des-mona, or whatever her name is."

"Doesn't bother me," I said, laughing. But it did seem right for us, because I understand Othello. And Dean is as beautiful as Desdemona ever was.

"Can you embroider?" he asked.

"No. But I'll learn to. Just for you."

He folded his arms. "So how does it all turn out?"

"The play? Oh. Well, it's a tragedy, of course. So you can't expect . . . I mean. Well—uh, he kills her actually."

"Othello? Kills Des-mona?"

I felt foolish now. "He does love her though. Really. Right to the end."

"Sick," Dean said. "So sick."

"No, no. You don't understand. It was because of Iago. And all the lies he kept telling." There I was, Jessie—do you believe it? Making excuses for Shakespeare!

"I don't even want to hear, Carla. It's too creepy. Just skip the strawberries, okay? And keep the hankie. I have lots more." He looked at his watch. "Say, I'll definitely have to leave by five. What about you?"

"I can stay that long. Dad has an open house till six."

"How 'bout trying your present on?"

"I can't. With this sweater, it wouldn't fit around my neck."

Dean gave me a mischievous look. "You could take it off though—I mean, the sweater. Nobody can see in here."

I braced myself. "Dean I'd better not. I don't feel that well today and—"

"I won't bother you or anything. If that's what's stopping you. And it sure is warm enough in here. Too warm actually."

"I'm embarrassed," I said.

"Well, you may be shy," he said. "But I'm not." He

151

unbuttoned his shirt, managing to make even that mundane action look graceful. Then he took the shirt off and folded it with scrupulous care, placing it on the floor beside us.

"I've seen you without your shirt before," I told him playfully.

"I know. At the beach that time. But in here doesn't it seem—you know, a little more daring somehow?"

I looked at his velvety skin and the beginnings of black hair on his chest and his slender arms. I really wanted to touch him, but I couldn't because then my scratchy sweater would only seem that much more in the way.

"Come on, Carla. I promise I won't do anything but look. I'm not exactly your standard sex maniac, you know. I just want to see you with your necklace on."

And I thought about it, Jessie. The muted lamplight seemed unlikely to expose my secrets. Better here than outdoors in the daylight, where later Dean might insist on trying to put the chain around my neck. And my refusal might be harder to justify.

"I want to see it on you," he said patiently.

And I thought that surely he wouldn't be able to see the marks or scars in this near darkness. And I was yearning for the feel of his beloved body next to mine. I pulled off my sweater and, in what had to be an absurd parody of his own movements, folded the moth-eaten bulk of it and put it aside. When I looked up again, his hand was covering his mouth.

I fought panic. "What's wrong?"

"God, you're so thin." The tips of his thumb and forefinger strayed into his mouth. "I just don't believe it."

Irritation caught me, not to mention relief. "Come on, Dean. Don't."

"I'm sorry. But, Carla, you've got to build up again."

I can't stand it when he gets like this, more hawk eyed

152

and preachy than your own conscience. But at least he was only noticing my weight loss. I unhooked the clasp of my new necklace.

When I looked up again, it was obvious that Dean's anxiety hadn't subsided. "You lost *all* that weight in ten days?"

"Most of it." Arms raised above my head, I tried to clasp the necklace. Oddly, I wasn't feeling self-conscious at all now about my nakedness.

"What have you been living on?" he said heavily. "Air? Or what?"

Still struggling with the necklace, I smiled at him. "Love."

He moved closer and reached around my neck to help me. "Don't blame this on love," he said, "or I'd have to say I'm really bad for you."

"Dean—don't make a big deal, okay? Don't wreck things."

On his knees now, he'd clasped the necklace, and before I could stop him, he lifted the lamp to my neck for a closer look. But I didn't pull away from him in time, or casually enough. He put down the lamp. Then he rubbed his eyes, pushing deeply into the closed lids. For an instant I could almost pretend that it hadn't happened.

Until Dean's hands fluttered down into his lap. After a long moment he said, "I'm going to ask you a question. Even though I know you're going to want to lie."

I was struggling to breathe normally.

"So answer or don't answer, all right? But just don't lie." He took a deep breath. "How did you get those marks on your neck?"

In my own lame way, I played for time. "I don't know."

He raised his finger and jabbed at the air between us. "Lie! Try again."

I didn't know him now. "Please," I said.

His eyes suddenly filled. "Please what? Don't ask you who tried to strangle you? What do you think I am, Carla? A dummy?"

"No. I mean, it isn't what you think."

He chewed on his fingertips again. "Hey, look. My mom worked the emergency room for two years. Yeah. And she used to tell me all these stories."

I shook my head ineffectually, trying to fend him off, and the ever-increasing pressure.

"She'd tell me about kids beaten up so bad they couldn't move. And if they were conscious enough to be questioned they never would say what happened. Or they'd tell a lie so phony it was almost laughable."

Feeling light-headed now, I laid a comforting hand against my throat.

"That hurts, doesn't it?" he said woodenly. "I'm starting to get it now. The pain pill begins to make sense."

My sweater looked appealingly familiar, and I stroked it for a moment, then picked it up. I would put it on. I would leave. Because the quiet force of Dean's anger was terrifying. I would not wait for it to overwhelm me.

Still holding the sweater, I touched the silver strawberry. "I love this," I whispered. "I'm sorry."

Then he was holding out his arms to me. I dropped the sweater and he held me again. But delicately this time, as though he thought he might hurt me. I kissed the place I like most, the warm place just under his chin, and kept my lips there for a long time.

He shook his head. "I was hoping to tell you about my plan, Carla. Not like this, of course. No. But it was a way we could get out of where we are and live together. Work and go to college and all. You're old enough now that we could do it."

I liked the soothing sound of his voice. The pain in my

154

chest began to ease a little, and I was breathing more freely again.

"You know," he went on, "get a real small apartment for just the two of us. In one of those cheap neighborhoods. With another roommate if we have to. Or even a couple more if we have to. Get a place near City College 'cause it's the least expensive school, and we could swing it all ourselves. Go to night school and work days. Or the opposite. No welfare or anything, except food stamps. We couldn't make it without them probably. And I'm still on my Mom's health insurance and you're probably on his. And if not, you could apply for Medi-Cal. I know all about that stuff. But the main thing we'd be on our own. Making our own life."

I couldn't tell him that the things he was talking about were incomprehensible to me: welfare and food stamps and Medi-Cal. They drifted over my head like foreign words in the soft, depressed tone that woman sometimes used so long ago. That Mrs. Andrews.

"But it's all different now," he said. "Because you can't wait till school's out. No—this is a whole other thing."

"What is?" I asked, feeling like a baby in his arms, liking even the stickiness of our skin together in the warm air.

"You. I mean, I'm not a complete idiot, Carla. I may have been pretty slow about things in the past, but I know who did this to you. And that's all, okay? It's the end."

Our skin came unstuck as I moved back from him a little. "The end? Of what?"

"Him! The bastard ought to be locked up somewhere. But right now the main thing is you. You being safe."

Why was my head so muddy just then? "Safe?"

"I'll call Mom from the library," he said thoughtfully, and it didn't seem as if he was talking to me anymore. "No, better yet—I'll call Sid, our house parent. And he'll know where I can take you after the hospital."

"Take me?" I was starting to catch on, and alarm clutched at my insides. "Dean, wait. I don't need to go anywhere."

"Yeah." He was unruffled, firm. "You do. There has to be a shelter or something. But first we get you checked out. Make sure you're okay."

"No. I mean, you're making all these plans. And it isn't necessary, Dean."

"Carla? How long has he been pulling stuff like this?" Then, without waiting, he said, "The whole time. Sure."

"You don't understand."

"Oh, no? What's to understand? I mean, your own father is doing this to you. Only you aren't going to let it happen anymore. Or he'll wind up killing you. I didn't mention that part of my mom's stories. The dead ones."

I can't say why, Jessie, but my principal feeling at that moment was shame. "He wouldn't," I said.

"Oh, yeah?"

"He never has."

"Sure. Great. Fantastic. And he won't get one more fucking chance to either. Hey—I'm sorry. I didn't mean to use that word."

Oh, my innocent one, you never lose your power to move me. "Don't worry."

"No wonder you're not eating," he went on dully. "God."

I brought his hand to my lap, caressing it with both of my own. How he cares about me, I thought. And for a moment I was strangely happy.

"I mean, all this time, Carla. I've known damn well he was lying through his teeth. Sure. About everything. Your entire past. All that funny stuff about your birth certificate getting burned up and all. I tried to tell you before how preposterous that is. Birth records get sent to the state health department or somewhere—vital statistics.

They just don't stay there in the hospital where you were born. And that baptism certificate he flashes around. I mean, I'm not Catholic or anything, but I bet anybody could phony up a deal like that. If he says that certificate is the straight scoop, then it's probably a lie. And the way he says he burned those pictures of your mother. Bull, Carla. How gullible can you be? If he did get rid of them, it was to cover something up. Because things like that just don't happen in real life. I guess you've probably seen this yourself all along. You've just been scared out of your mind."

But I haven't seen it that way, Jessie. And I still don't.

"You're getting out of there, okay? Right now. Forget about clothes and stuff. I know I can get you fixed up with something. Let's go over to my place and talk to Sid about it."

"No—we can't do that!"

He was staring at me. "Maybe you're willing to take another chance on getting killed. But I won't let you."

I got to my feet. "I'm going home, Dean. Like always."

He stood up, too. "Oh, yeah? Well, the way things are going you'll be dead in a month. Or a week. You look like death already. God, I wish I'd been around you more lately. Have you checked a mirror? And this guy chokes you, for God's sake. Chokes you hard enough to leave marks like those. This is the kind of thing they write about in newspapers. You act like it's okay."

I was afraid now, Jessie. He was acting the way he did just before he wouldn't speak to me that time. Only now it was worse.

"They'll take pictures of your neck at the hospital. And then you can nail him."

But I knew I would never go to any hospital. "They wouldn't believe me," I argued.

"Why not?"

"He'll say someone else did it. I don't know. A stranger maybe."

"I don't get it." Dean looked worried now. "You mean, your word against his and all?"

I nodded.

"But I'll tell them, too, Carla. I mean, I've known you for over a year."

I knew I was getting somewhere at last. "But what can you tell them? You've never even met him."

"So? I know he's been keeping you in that jail."

"How do you know? For sure, I mean? Because I know what he will say. That I'm crazy and talk to myself and make up stories. That all you know is what you've heard from me. He'll say I'm nuts—he says that sometimes already—and he can charm people, Dean. You haven't met him. He's a salesman, and he's fantastic at it. He has friends who'll speak up for him. They'll say he's a wonderful person. One of them's a priest, Dean. A Catholic priest. And another one's a doctor."

"I didn't get the impression your father is that social."

"He isn't. He doesn't entertain people at our house or anything. He goes out with them. Drinking. And sometimes he drops in and has a toddy with Monsignor Dailey. He's real proud of that. Monsignor Dailey likes my Dad so much he gave him a bottle of whiskey he smuggled back from Ireland last year. You don't know my father. And take Bucky Hogan. He's been around Dad for seven or eight years and thinks he's the salt of the earth. I mean, I've heard Bucky use those very words."

"But he isn't, dammit. He tried to kill you!"

"He didn't mean to, though. I mean, not really. He gets mad sometimes. Carried away."

Dean was actually wringing his hands. "God, Carla, did you hear what you just said? The bastard tried to strangle you!"

158

I covered his agonized hands with my own again. "But I can't do anything about it. My Dad was even in the Knights of Columbus at Saint Agatha's. He coached Pop Warner football for three years in a row. I remember how it goes from before when Dad almost got married. I was twelve and there was this widow named Velma Saunders. She owned a wig shop and she was really nice. For a while it was looking good, but then something happened. I'm not too sure about it all, except I started my period the first time and Velma helped me with what to do and she noticed some marks on me or something. Asked me about them, too, only I didn't tell her anything. But she looked at me real funny and a little while later she was at our apartment late one night and I heard her scream. Just once—it was really weird—and then it got real quiet. And I heard her leave. About two days later this caseworker came to our house to check on me. Dad always said that Velma must have sent her. To get even or something because they broke up. And I never did see Velma again."

"What did the caseworker do?"

"I guess she was talking to Dad alone or something. I didn't even know she was in the apartment that day. And when I went into the kitchen to start dinner, the caseworker saw me go by. Dad looked embarrassed 'cause he'd told her I was at a Girl Scout meeting or something. But this lady got me alone right away and asked me a bunch of questions. I didn't tell her anything because I'd never get my Dad into trouble. I was really scared."

"It's been going on all this time," he said.

I nodded. "So don't worry. I'm not going to get killed."

His eyes were suddenly luminous. "You're dying right now."

I put my hand over his mouth, but he pulled it away.

159

"What happened?" he asked. "Did the caseworker catch on?"

"No. Even after she caught Dad in that fib about my not being home. And me, I was shaking like a leaf the whole time I was with her. But at the end she talked to Dad alone again. At one point I even heard her laughing with him. Anyway she left finally and that was the last of her, too."

"But that won't happen this time, Carla. 'Cause you're not going back there at all. Even if we have to run away."

"He'd find us, Dean. And he'd go after you for sure."

"I don't care."

"I do. He has about sixty pounds on you, at least. And he used to be a policeman."

"That says a lot for L.A.'s finest."

"No. Not here. It must have been somewhere else. A few years ago."

"This is just too incredible. He's probably lying about that, too. To keep you scared of him or something. I always knew that guy was nuts—just from what you said about him. But I never thought—"

"Look, Dean. There are two sides to everything, right? Like a lot of this is my fault. I know him and his temper. But I still give him a hard time."

"You're blaming *yourself*?"

"I get him going, that's all. Challenge him."

"You?" He laughed harshly. "You're about as rebellious as a Twinkie."

I persisted. "Just take my word, Dean. A lot of the problem is me."

"I think I must be hearing things. I really do. Does he have marks on his neck? Have you tried to strangle him lately? What is this?"

"It's his temper. Mostly when he's drinking."

Dean's look was sardonic. He pulled at one of his fingernails with his teeth. "Carla, he's the adult here. You're supposed to be the kid. You're making excuses for him like he was two."

"In some ways he is."

"I can't believe we're having this conversation. That I'm actually in some kind of argument here. I'm going to call my mom. Or maybe Sid would be better. Or both of them. I guess I'd like Mom because we could maybe go to the hospital where she's working now. If she's on duty. Because you don't have any insurance stuff on you and you're underage."

I moved away from him and reached for my sweater. "No, Dean. I won't go. I'm not turning my father in. He'd just end up having me put away."

"He can't just have you put away. It doesn't work like that. If somebody did a psych workup on him they'd find out how completely nuts *he* is."

"Dad would never take a test like that, Dean. He hates psychologists worse than anything."

Dean was glaring at me now. "I'll bet he does. So you think you're going back there, put in more time as a human punching bag. Wrong. I'll turn him in to the police myself. The minute you leave here."

"You can't."

"I will."

Never, I thought desperately. "It won't work. I'll deny it. Everything."

I'm still trying to forget the look that came into his eyes just then. He picked up his shirt and slowly put it on, his eyes like lead. "Well, you got me there," he said. "I guess you win." He leaned back and, in slow motion, stretched his legs out in front of him. "Sure, you do," he added softly.

I squeezed the silver charm until it bit into my fingers.

"If you go back to that house today, it's over for us, Carla. That's it."

As though on cue, my throat flared with pain, and I felt myself moving downward through it, searching for the numbness at the core.

"You've already betrayed me," he said. "All this time pretending to be honest. Letting me love you. Maybe it isn't fair to say that—or selfish even—but I can't help it. I'm not going to be around when he kills you. I may not be much, but I just don't deserve that."

Still holding the sweater in my foolish hands, I turned to stone.

"You have to go now," he said. "I don't want you here anymore."

I would rather that he'd hit me. I would have preferred to be dead.

"You want this I guess. Something in you. Otherwise you'd fight."

The paralysis drained away from me and I stood up wearily.

"Are you going?" His voice was suddenly pitched higher. "You are."

Then he was on his feet, too, pulling me toward him. I stood, holding the sweater rigidly between us to keep him at a distance, to protect myself.

"I love you, Carla. Get it? I don't want you hurt at all. Not even a little bit. What do you expect me to feel about this?"

I knew I had to go. Before my poison spread further, before it seeped into Dean and ruined him forever.

Then all at once he erupted with: "Carla, what about your other relatives? If you could find one, even one, I bet you'd get some help. They can't all be like him? What about your mother's folks? If you could find *them*, I mean. I'll bet they'd give anything to see you. I mean, their daughter dies. Then their granddaughter disappears. God, Carla, think about that."

But I already have, Jessie, especially when I was younger. Sometimes I'd think about that for hours. Now anxiety twisted inside me. "I don't know how to find them."

"There's got to be a clue around somewhere. Think, Carla. A record of some kind. Some sort of connection with your past. People don't just disappear without a trace like that, like in some lousy movie. The way he's gotten rid of the evidence it's almost like he kidnapped you or something."

And I've thought about that, too, Jessie. Then, requiring some relief, I've cut myself. Just a little.

Desperately eager now, Dean pressed on. "Like a safe deposit box in a bank. Or a safe. A strongbox somewhere. My mom has always had one for important papers—marriage licenses, birth certificates and stuff. She used to keep it under her bed. Does he have anything like that?"

Caught off guard, I said uneasily, "In his desk at home. I saw it once in the bottom drawer. At least it used to be there. But I'm sure he keeps it locked. And the desk, too."

Dean's dark eyes glowed. "Where are the keys?"

"On his key ring."

"Then you've got to get them."

"No," I said. "Too scary."

"Hell, Carla! Don't you see? Your life isn't even worth living right now. This might be the way out."

"What if he catches me?"

"You'll have to be careful. Really super careful. And I'll be waiting for you right outside your house. If you don't come out when you're supposed to, I'll ring the doorbell and stop whatever might be going on." He grinned. "I'll be a magazine salesman. Or a Jehovah's Witness or something. No sweat."

I played my only ace. "He's got a gun."

Dean looked startled. "Now that isn't so good." He scratched his head. "Okay, okay. How can you get it?"

"When he's out. I could get it then. But why?"

"Because if he should happen to hear you, what's the first thing he'd reach for?"

I respected his foresight.

Dean hugged me. "Carla, did you hear yourself just now? You're helping. You're into it. Now what if he notices the gun is gone? Not likely, but just in case."

"I'll say I'm cleaning it."

"You know how?"

"Sure. It's a little time-consuming. But not that hard."

Dean was incredulous again. "He teach you?"

I nodded self-consciously, feeling completely naked now.

"The man is so weird," he said. "I don't even want to know how weird he is."

No, I thought. You don't.

"All right," he said, businesslike again. "So it's set for tonight."

"Oh, no, Dean. Not so soon. I mean, it's Saturday. He'll be out at the bar. I can never tell how late. He could walk right in on me.

"Do it after he gets home, okay? With luck he might even be polluted or something. Wait till he goes to sleep. Till he's really out. And then you're on."

It hit me now. That Dean was serious about this. And convinced as usual that he could talk me into anything. "I can't."

"Yes, you can, Carla. Because if you don't do it to-night, then *I'll* do something."

No, I thought. "Like what?"

"Like talk to him myself. Tell him what I know. Tell him I'll be watching him."

Of course, my father would be about as frightened of Dean as he would of a mouse. But what could I say?

Dean guessed what was on my mind. "Look, I know you think that's funny, Carla. But I don't care. I'll do it. And if he tries anything with me, I'll go to the cops. Besides, I know what your problem is. You're afraid of what you'll find out. I mean, that box has been there for a while, hasn't it? Probably years. It doesn't take a genius to figure you should have checked it out long ago. And you happen to be a genius, in my humble opinion. Only you want to keep it quiet, too, Carla, because you're as scared of the facts as he is."

Dean's accuracy aroused in me a peculiar blend of fury and relief. "I'm not going to find out a thing, Dean. Not one single thing."

He smiled shrewdly. "Fine, then. There's no problem."

The close, warm air in the van was nauseating me. "Let's go."

"Not till you agree to the plan. If it doesn't happen tonight, I'll do what I said. I'll be over to see him first thing in the morning." Dean grinned impishly. "I'll mix his Bloody Mary myself."

My heart contracted. "How do you know he drinks Bloody Marys?"

"I didn't. But I'm not surprised or anything. I imagine he's about as predictable as a toad."

"You don't have to say things like that."

"I do if I want to keep from exploding."

So there I was, Jessie. Surrounded. Ambushed. And realizing even then that I'd somehow brought it on myself.

Feeling sick inside, I agreed to the plan.

Dean walked me part way home, polishing tonight's details with the enthusiasm of a secret agent. He would be parked near the front of my house from about two in the morning on. When Dad fell asleep I'd take the key ring from his bureau, go downstairs and turn on the porch light to signal Dean that the plan was in effect.

Then I would go to Dad's office, unlock the desk and the strongbox. I'd make fast notes from whatever papers I found there, return them to the box, lock it and the desk, and return the keys to their place. When the porch light went out, Dean would know I'd be meeting him within ten minutes. If he saw a light in my Dad's bedroom or if I took more than the allotted time to arrive, he'd come to the front door right away. When my father answered it, Dean would tell him some story about having car trouble.

Even with all that, Jessie, he didn't want to let me go.

"I hate this," he said. "I feel like I'm sending you back to the evil tower and this time you'll be locked up in there forever. . . ."

"Like Rapunzel?"

That brought a half-smile. "Yeah."

I told him at least a dozen times that I was okay and convinced him that I could make it home on my own today, and then he finally let me go.

But as soon as I was on my way, Jessie, panic took root. And all I could see was Dean poised outside our house in the darkness, my father inside with his careless, angry lust. The two of them so close together, terrifyingly close.

When I've always known I must keep them far apart.

That is, if we are all to survive.

I am distraught, Jessie. I am beside myself.

I have been reckless and now must pay the price.

Daddy, *please* believe me.

I'd rather die than get you in trouble.

Oh, God—what have I done?

I reach for another pill. All at once craving that infallible release.

Then I say: No, traitor.
You may not be delivered from your pain.

I look at my necklace in the mirror.
All around it the marks from my father's hands are darkening.
But the silver strawberry lies in the hollow of my throat and it is still beautiful.

I have the gun now. Hidden far down inside my sleeping bag where he can't find it. My father didn't come home at all this evening, so I had plenty of time to take his gun to my room for safekeeping.
I'm here now, Jessie, on the floor, half under my quilt, writing to you. My book of Emily's poetry is visible from under the bed and my dear companions are all around me. They know, of course. They know about the trouble.
And Max is so frightened.
He is a sensitive mouse, not a brave one.
Hush, little one. My Max. Mymouse. Hush, sweet baby—sh-h-h.

A temptation. Hanging like a strawberry ripe and sweet before my mouth.
It would be so easy. And I wouldn't get caught.
Yes. I've just thought of something shameful, Jessie. A thoroughly unscrupulous way out of tonight. To concoct a story for Dean. A story of what I found in a strongbox I never opened at all.
The lie to end all lies.
Am I a natural liar then? What they call a pathological liar? To the manner born, as it were?

I could do it surely, only what would it mean? That Dean is right about everything? That I'm scared to death of what I'll find?

No, it can't be. The papers in that box are surely as dry as dead moths: life insurance, stocks, and other indecipherable things. And if I go ahead with this as agreed, Dean will be satisfied. At least for now. I will have done my duty honestly.

My duty? Is that what I call this piece of blackmail? From someone who says he loves me?

They're ruling me now, Jessie—both of them. Perhaps there is something in the masculine voice that makes me cower. Certainly there is in my father's. But in Dean's? Yes, I think so. Not so much in the firmness of it, but in the caring.

As it turns out then, Dean's love makes him a tyrant like my father.

I know what you're thinking. You're on Dean's side of things. And you're smiling because I balk at this invasion, to be carried out with malice of forethought, of my father's privacy. You find my reluctance ironic. Manipulative even. Another smoke screen.

Your insights torment me. Your unending concern for me is the final tyranny.

Will I ever escape from other people's ideas of what I should be?

You accept no argument. Mine is no longer to reason why. I've somehow lost that right. Carla—the human punching bag. The washed-out fighter with brains like mush and a broken face.

Of course, I'm afraid of tonight, Jessie. You and Dean both know that.

But I will open the strongbox.

168

And if one "i" isn't dotted the way my father says it should be, I will come apart.

The phone rang a few minutes ago and it was Dad. He made a big sale today and chattered on about the size of the commission and our future in the Palisades. A celebration is happening now at the Silver Mine Saloon. Dad will be home, as usual, in the small hours of the morning.

His daughter lies in wait for him.

Dean's two-ring signal came at 1:27 A.M. by my digital clock. He was calling to report that he's half a mile from here in a phone booth and has Sid's car and so far, so good. I told him I could carry out our plan quite effectively without his babysitting in front of my house. He ignored me. I then explained that Dad would be home shortly after two, but since he's so excited about the day's success and all, he probably wouldn't be getting to sleep for a while after that.

Dean assured me that his patience has no limits. A typical Dean overstatement and, as usual, quite annoying.

Jessie, do you ever ask yourself why I put up with him? My stubborn difficult demanding know-it-all Dean? And why I trust him?

Well, I've already figured it out. I've decided that if Dean's love isn't true, then nothing else would matter anyway.

All would be meaningless.

My father altered his routine tonight; he brought Bucky home for a nightcap. Dad even called up to me from the bottom of the stairs to ask if I wanted to join them. When I didn't answer, he went away.

Right now their cheerfully boisterous sounds are filling the house. A ballad of old Ireland. I can tell from my father's voice, thickly sentimental and wavering off-key, that he isn't far from passing out.

At last the house is still. There is peace, even purity, in its silence. I heard Bucky leave and my father come upstairs to his room. He moved slowly, humming the song he and Bucky had shared earlier.

I turn toward my clock, watching its green numerals bleeping each minute away in the darkness. I will wait for at least half an hour. At three-thirty, I will make my move.

My bedroom windows are open. I'd hoped to hear Dean's car pull up in front before, but I didn't. Still, I know he is there.

I wonder how he could bear to touch me today. His skin is so soft. There is only a little hair on his body. His arms are smaller than Dad's, his stomach much flatter. He is young. Submissive and blind as a lamb.

And I am filth. How could he not notice?

When he held me, he didn't breathe fast and heavy the way Dad does. And I didn't breathe that way either. I never do. Because I feel nothing. Just like the girls in Dad's photos and movies. Those girls who are saying to themselves: I am numb. Waiting for it to be over.

Just like me.

But my father doesn't see that. He concentrates on making one thing happen. Gets angry when it happens too soon. Furious when it doesn't happen at all.

170

Dean and I held each other today and my nipples touched his bare chest. His body is small and clean.

You won't believe me when I say this, Jessie, but tonight I have made a sacred vow.

My father will never touch me again.

Emily Dickinson knew.

> This is the hour of lead
> Remembered if outlived
> As freezing persons recollect
> the snow—
> First chill, then stupor, then
> The letting go.

I do it all. Slave and robot that I am. I stand listening in the boozy darkness of my father's room. He is sprawled naked on the bed and I can smell the urine that has seeped from his ungoverned bladder. And I know that the stench of him has crept into the very walls.

His key ring is not on the bureau where it belongs.

His discarded clothing is heaped into the big bedroom chair. I sort through it soundlessly and slip my hand into his pants pockets.

I remove the keys.

Hating Dean all the time, Jessie. And hating you.

I creep downstairs, a thief in my own house. Poised for a long uncertain moment at the front room window, I finally pull aside enough drapery to see out. And it is there across the street to my left, the old green VW Dean promised. The car is facing away from our house, and though the street is awash in moonlight, I can't see Dean inside.

I move into the front hall and turn on the porch light—our signal.

I am committed now to the task. My father's office is a

171

converted out-of-the-way laundry room off our kitchen. I enter the small windowless room, closing the door carefully behind me. I grope for the light, sit down in the comfortable swivel chair. Another of my father's seats of power. I have never been in this room before, the result of a tacit understanding between him and me. I lay his key ring on the blotter and pull a tablet out of my back pocket.

It is a safe, quiet place to violate my father's trust.

The beat of my heart moves up into my beleaguered throat. My damp fingers are awkward as they manipulate the keys. Still I manage to unlock the desk and bring the strongbox up out of the bottom drawer.

My fingers tremble over the lock. I suddenly envision my father bursting through the door, his powerful drunken body upon me.

But there is only silence.

I wait for my pulse to slow. Dean's voice taunts me: *You're afraid, afraid 'cause you don't want to know.*

And I hate him. I'm not afraid. And I will prove it.

The intelligent Carla Jean Hughes—suckered by a juvenile dare.

The chill that Emily spoke of—I am feeling it now.

Daddy—I'm sorry.

The box is half-filled with papers. On top is the title to our house. Under that an equally uninteresting life insurance policy. Then fire insurance papers. I lay each document face down on the desk to the left of the strongbox, planning to replace them exactly as I find them. The circumspection of larceny.

There is a stock certificate. It appears that my father has ten shares in the steel company he once worked for. I lift out the certificate. And then I see it.

A photograph. Black and white. Wallet size. So incongruous in this setting.

A very ordinary photograph of a young couple at what

172

looks to be a school dance. A callow-looking Carl Jay Hughes, Jr., with a girl no older than I am. I hold the photograph up close to the lamp, peer at it hungrily. She has short, dark hair in a style that looks artificial, old-fashioned. Her smile is girlishly confident; in any era she would be considered pretty. And more—she has the look of one who is loved. My father's face reflects carefully restrained pride. His hair is angelically light, his face the "honest" one that has carried him so far.

On the back of the photograph in my father's hand-writing are the words: Jean and Jay.

I am frustrated, wanting to see much more than the photograph shows. I lay it down, my fingers lingering there, unwilling to break contact.

A lie, my father. That you burned every picture of my mother. When you could have shown me this one all along.

I imagine Dean's face. Dean Lowrey. Vindicated so soon.

But perhaps—did my father just forget about this picture?

I can hear Dean's derisive hoot.

I turn the photograph over and place it on the pile of already-scrutinized material.

Next in the box is my baptismal certificate, which I have seen before. From Saint Agatha's Church in Los Angeles. Baptized by the Rt. Reverend Stephen P. Dailey eight years ago: Carla Jean Hughes, born October 12. Godparents: Robert Hogan and Rayette M. Osborn (Bucky's girlfriend at the time). I remember, Jessie. Monsignor Dailey said, "Go out of her, you unclean spirit, and give place to the Holy Spirit . . . I exorcise you, unclean spirit, in the name of God the Father almighty . . ." And Rayette made a big dinner afterward, and I thought it all meant my father wouldn't hurt me anymore.

I lift out the baptismal certificate and lay it down.

Now I am looking at a second baptismal certificate, which I assume at first to be my father's.

No. It is dated October 7 of the year before I was born. And I see the name.

The stupor, Jessie. When life quickens no longer, and there is only a mute and languid drift.

My right hand reaches for the tablet, records the bewildering date and even more bewildering name. For it seems that there is another Carla. Not Carla Jean Hughes, and not the child of Carl Jay Hughes, Jr., and Jean Mallory Hughes.

More than a year before I was born, a Carla Inger Hughes, child of Carl Jay Hughes, Jr., and Birgitta Arneson Hughes, was baptized. My hand, efficient, disembodied, moves on. Carla Inger Hughes, born in the city of Longfield, the county of Norman, the state of New Jersey, on the twenty-seventh day of September.

I turn another page of my tablet and write: St. Gregory's Church, 171 Allen Street, Longfield, NJ.

I am struck by a moment of intense nausea. *Longfield.* Where nothing ever happens.

Oh, yes, yes, Dad. Longfield. Where the life of a policeman is consummately dull.

The nausea passes and I am comforted by the feel of the pen in my hand. I write: "Baptismal sponsors— Robert Dale Hughes and Triona Mary Hughes." Also names I know. Each dismissed over the years by a sentence or two. My Uncle Robbie and Aunt Tree. Robbie characterized as a "sap who doesn't set one foot out of the old man's front door" and Tree "who works in Las Vegas as a 'model,' if you know what I mean, Carly."

The sap and the model pressed into service as godparents for a phantom child—one Carla Inger Hughes.

The certificate signed by the Rt. Rev. John H. Snyder. The pastor from my Dad's early life.

I lifted out this certificate, too, and, still holding it, looked back into the box. Now I find a certificate of live birth. For one Carla Inger Hughes. The document intact, uncharred by the legendary hospital "fire."

My fingers quicken over my notes.

"Female. Single birth." And again, a birth date of September 27, the year before I thought I was born. Carla Inger Hughes born at 5:25 P.M. in Longfield Hospital, 118 Main Street, Longfield, NJ. "Maiden name of mother: Birgitta Elise Arneson. Birthplace: Minnesota. Age: 20. Name of father: Carl Jay Hughes, Jr. Birthplace: New Jersey. Age: 21.

I am writing as fast as I can.

At the bottom of the birth certificate I see her small, neat signature: "Birgitta E. Hughes."

I trace the signature with my fingertip. My heart contracts.

The physician signs with more flair: "Peter J. Colby, M.D."

And under that a marriage license, just as Dean predicted. Which tells me that my father married Birgitta Arneson on March 20 of the year Carla Inger Hughes was born. He is identified as a high school graduate, a police officer, and the son of Carl Jay Hughes, Sr., and Irma Lee Grollman. Birgitta's last occupation is listed as waitress, her last grade of schooling completed, the tenth. Her parents are Gunnar J. Arneson and Inger Ellen Lindstrom. The birthplace of both, Sweden.

My father's familiar signature appears at the bottom, and hers again, Birgitta's.

And that's all, Jessie. The marriage license at the bottom of the strongbox, the last document for me to see.

You will be proud of me because I keep my head. I put everything back just the way it was. In an exercise of zombielike detachment.

I turn out the light and leave my father's office.

For there are things to do.

First, of course, there is Dean.

I must get him away from here tonight. And back where he belongs.

I remember to turn off the porch light.

As I open the front door and move out into the street, I am not afraid. The cool night air sweeps refreshingly over my clammy skin. I see Dean watching for me now. He leans over, opens the door of the VW on the passenger side.

I get in. The car has a heavy, sweetish smell, as of food.

He grabs my hands. "Carla—are you okay?"

I nod. It is clear that I am much calmer than he is.

"When I saw that light go off, I knew you were safe. But I kept right on shaking."

It's true; I see that he is trembling even now. "It went fine." I smile at him. "No problems."

"God, you really did it! What did you find?"

"Nothing. At least nothing I haven't already seen before. Just insurance papers. Things like that. And my baptismal certificate." You see, Jessie, I am an actor. I know what to do.

There are circles under his dark eyes, and his disappointment touches me. "Nothing? Not even his marriage license?"

I shake my head, wanting to leave, becoming afraid of his presence, his emotion.

His fingers tighten on my arm. "He must keep the secret stuff somewhere else then. Like a safe deposit box. He might have figured you'd try to snoop."

No, never, Dean. My father is nothing if not confident.

I say, "Maybe, Dean. But I'd better go for right now."

"Go?" He looks stunned. "Back to him?"

"For tonight," I say smoothly. "We can talk about everything tomorrow."

"Come with me now," he pleads.

I know if I stay any longer the possibility exists that I could weaken. "The night's almost over now. He's sleeping it off. Tomorrow he'll be in bed for hours. Right up till he has to go to work."

Dean's face is tight with anger. "I want you out of there."

"I know. But he'd just come after us. We have to plan it out so he can't find me."

A touch of suspicion in his look. "You seem different, Carla."

"I do?"

"Yeah. I don't know. In some crazy way, you seem more sure of yourself."

About this at least, I can be honest. "I am. I'm on the move now."

"I guess it's the first time you've ever gone against him. Right?"

"Right." I check my watch; it's after four in the morning. "I've got to go, Dean. It would be awful to get caught now."

He sighs. "You make us sound like criminals or something. You have a right to know these things."

"Call me tomorrow afternoon," I tell him, touching the door handle.

"Why not in the morning?"

"We both need to sleep, Dean. Okay?"

"Okay, but I'm going to talk to Sid first thing tomorrow. He'll help us plan." Dean sees my panicked look. "What are you worried about? Sid will keep it cool."

"Hey, I did what you wanted tonight, didn't I. So take

it easy on me now, Dean. Give me a chance to breathe a little."

He looks embarrassed. "All right. I'm sorry. I don't want to put you in any worse danger. But I'm anxious about it, that's all."

I open the car door. "It'll be okay. It will."

"Well—all right." He reaches into the back seat. "Wait one minute. I brought you something. I figured you'd be hungry."

The sack is from a local doughnut shop.

"I thought you might like this." He offers me a cream puff. "It's a little wilted now because it's been in the car so long. But I'll bet it's still good."

I wrap the sticky thing in a couple of napkins. "Why a cream puff?"

"The calories," he says. "I know it isn't that healthy. But think of the calories."

The smell of cream puff permeates our small space. I move close to him. We kiss.

"I love you," he says softly. "Don't forget."

I move away from him again, then lean down and bring his hand up to my lips. I kiss it most tenderly, then force myself to let it go. I slide out of the car.

Good-bye, my love.

My dove.

My beautiful one.

Good-bye.

Who am I? Carla Inger Hughes?

If so, I don't know how to pronounce my own middle name. Perhaps it is "injure." As in, to injure. The urge to do grave bodily harm.

It seems that I was born on September 27 eighteen years ago.

I am a legal adult. Ready to put away the things of a child.

Only I have never been a child. Nor can I be an adult. I dwell in a limbo of mutants. A freak who has done everything, yet knows nothing.

At least I am not afraid anymore. I am calm. I am strong. I am the progeny of ruthlessness and deceit. This much I know. And I intend to know more.

I decide it will be safest to make the call from my father's office.

I go there, lay my notes out in front of me, and look at the telephone.

I find that I am no longer the weak-willed and sniveling Carla Jean Hughes. I am new. I am determined.

I lift the receiver and dial the local information operator, then learn how to dial information in Longfield, New Jersey. The operator there is a man. His accent generates a memory: Buck Hogan teasing my father about the way he talks, with an accent unlike that of a native Californian. I remember my father's startled look, his strangely defensive anger.

I ask for the number of St. Gregory's Church in Longfield. I ask for the time. I learn that in the state of New Jersey it is just after eight in the morning.

Ever my father's daughter, I have already put together a convincing story to get what I want.

The voice that says "St. Gregory's Church" belongs to an older woman.

I ask to speak with Father Snyder.

I am informed that he is saying the eight o'clock Mass.

I ask to leave a message. When she hears my name, the woman comes alive. "Who did you say?"

"Carla Hughes. I'll call back later."

"Not the granddaughter of Carl and Irma?"

"Yes," I say.

A moment passes before the woman speaks again. "I'm a good friend of theirs. Edith Bledsoe." She stops to clear her throat. "Have you called them, honey?"

"I don't know their number."

She gives it to me, along with their address. My right hand serenely does its duty. It all seems so easy now.

"I need to know some things," I say. "Maybe you could help me."

"Well—I will all I can. But why don't you talk to your grandmother? She'll—"

"I will, but could I talk to you first? Please?"

"Oh—well, I guess so."

"It's my father. He's ill. He's dying."

"Oh, Lord!"

"And he's been trying to tell me things about my past, but he isn't talking that well now. And I have a lot of questions."

"Honey, your grandmother should know about this. She's the one—"

"Please," I say tenaciously. "It's easier for me to talk to you right now. If you can understand."

"You mean, because I'm a stranger?"

I am grateful for this perception. "Yes." A stranger. Among strangers. "I wonder how long it's been—since you've seen my father. And me."

"Oh, let me see. It was before I started here as the rectory housekeeper. Eleven or twelve years ago, I'd say."

"What happened?" I ask.

"Well, it was so sad, dear. Your father letting on like he was taking you just for the weekend. You know, a trip to the shore, he said. Birgitta was real nervous anyway. She hated for you kids to be out of her sight. You were so young and all."

"We never came back."

"I know, honey, I know. Birgitta and Junior were separated at the time. And there'd been some trouble—I don't really know what it was. But it was supposed to be all straightened out. So she trusted Junior to take you. And she never forgave herself, Irma says."

I am dumb with joy. And I think: I didn't kill my mother.

I write it down: *My mother is alive.*

"Does she still live there?" I ask.

"Oh, no—no. Things got so bad for her here. She worked for a few months and then there were these spells she had sometimes. If it weren't for Max, I just don't know—"

"*Max?*"

"Your big brother, honey."

"Broder?"

"Well, now, that was some of your mother's Swedish talk. A nickname-like. But your brother's name was Max. A fine young man he is, too. Real good-hearted, just like his Mama. Twenty-one or two and in the service. Over in Europe now somewhere I think."

I am fighting to keep my voice under control. "My father never mentioned him."

"Well—there was that other problem—only I just don't feel right, dear. If you'd please talk to Irma about these things—"

"It's all right. I promise. It would only upset her anyway, wouldn't it?"

The woman is silent for a moment. "Well, she and I have been friends since we were kids. I guess she might understand. I hope so anyway."

"I'll let her tell me, too," I promise. "In her own way."

"Honey, you sound like a real nice girl. Irma's going to be so happy."

"Could you tell me more about the other problem?" I prod gently.

"Well, it was while Junior and Birgitta were in high school. And she got pregnant with Max. Only fifteen at the time, poor thing, and crazy in love with Junior even then. Only he just wouldn't accept that Max was his. Even though that boy turned out to be the spitting image of his daddy. Poor Birgitta. She and her mother had been struggling to make ends meet as it was. After a couple of years with the baby, her mother tried to get Birgitta to go back to the Midwest with her. But the girl just wouldn't budge. Wouldn't leave town as long as her Junior was there. So the mother just gave up on her and went back alone. Birgitta had to manage pretty much by herself after that."

Oh, Mama—your Carlek is here.

"Brigitta just kept waiting for Junior to grow up some, sow his wild oats and all, the way boys do. I guess she loved him the whole time. A real loyal little thing. And they finally did get married, surprised the whole town, and then they had you. What's wrong with him, honey? Is it cancer or something."

"Yes," I say with satisfaction. "A fast-moving cancer."

"At his age—land. It seems awful talking about him like this, sick as he is."

"It's all right though. He wants to tell me these things himself. But he just can't right now."

"Well, you haven't asked a word about your grandma and grandpa."

"How are they?" I ask, and I think: Who are they?

"Just fine. Carl has a little of that emphysema, I'm afraid. And Irma's arthritis really plagues her now and then. But they come from good farm stock, you know, and I'm sure they're going to last a long time."

"Where is my mother now?"

Silence. Then, "Please, why don't you talk to Irma, honey?"

"It's been so long, all this. I need to know now."

Another hesitation. I am beginning to be afraid. "She had these spells, honey, like I said. And she wouldn't come out of her little house for days. You could always tell because Max would look so scruffy going to school. Sometimes he didn't go to school at all."

My Max. Mymouse.

And I think: No, I can't let myself feel yet.

"Anyway, Irma came to the house one day and found Birgitta sitting in the middle of the kitchen floor. And she'd been cutting up newspapers and there were shreds of them all over. And they called Dr. Cahill and finally they sent Birgitta down to the state hospital in Trenton."

Oh, God, Mama. I'm so sorry.

I am exasperated. I am frightened. "But where is she *now?*"

"I'm getting to that, dear, but I have to explain it right. She did come home after a while and things went pretty well, I think, and then she ended up having to go back. Irma was always worried sick about her. And Irma'd end up taking care of Max herself half the time. Birgitta would get so downhearted she just couldn't. She was just forever looking for you. Wrote letters everywhere. Carl and Irma helped, too, but all I can say is, Junior must have worked it out real well. Planned it so careful and all. Because nobody could find hide nor hair of him. And the police just couldn't do that much, since he was your real father. To think nobody's heard a peep out of that man for all these years."

Terror and rage are building steadily inside me. "And my mother?"

"It shouldn't have been, honey. It just shouldn't. But she got so downhearted they took her back to that hospital, and something happened where they didn't keep

183

watch on her well enough. She got hold of this light bulb and broke it and—"

"*Please!*" I say. "Is she alive?"

"I'm sorry," the woman says, and I can barely hear her now. "No."

I lay down my pen and push away the tablet. After a long time I hear myself say, "I remember her. Her hair was all gold."

"Oh, she was a beauty," the woman says with awe. "In that Swedish way. And so were you. Birgitta always called you her little princess."

Then I say softly, "I have to go now."

"But, wait, honey—where are you calling from? What's your number? Irma'll be just desperate to talk to you."

"I'm sorry," I say again.

"Should Father offer up the Holy Sacrifice of the Mass then? For Junior?"

I cannot think any longer. I hang up the telephone.

I lay my head down on the desk and close my eyes, but I can still see. See myself sitting on Mama's lap as she tells me the story of the little princess.

"Her name was Bianca Maria. And she looked just like you, Carlek. Her eyes were big and blue and her little mouth turned up so sweetly and her skin was as delicate as the petal of a flower . . ."

Oh, Mama, I waited for you. I always waited, even after school when teacher said we could go home, and then on the way I walked slow so you wouldn't miss me. If you came it wouldn't of happened and I'd still be good and I'd still have Max.

But it happened. I'm almost home 'cause I'm in the alley where we live and the sky is all rainy gray and the air smells a little like garbage. Behind the grocery store I

184

see something move near the big trash cans and I stop to see it. There are some cardboard boxes that smell funny and I don't move till I see the other thing again. It's a black kitten, skinnier than me with four white feet and white on his neck and his front.

I know I want him, Mama, and I need to move real careful or he'll run away. Remember what you tell me? To make friends I have to *be* a animal. I like to be a kitty and I get down on my hands and move real quiet and a piece of broken glass bites my knee but I don't care. I stop every little while to look around just like a kitty does and when I get near him, he isn't even scared that I'm there. He's hanging over the edge of the box trying to get something and his baby claws make scratch noises on the box. And I just hold out my hands and take him and his claws go into my arms for a minute—not meanlike 'cause he's just scared—and then they stop.

I stand up with him and find a little box with a lid on and I go up the stairs to the place where Daddy and I live. And I put the kitty inside the box for just a minute and close the lid and put my foot on top and get the chain off my neck and unlock the door. I bring my kitty inside and let him out of the box right away so he can breathe. And he walks around the room and looks at everything and sniffs it all. Then I feed him some milk and clean him, and he gets all soft and goes to sleep right in my arms. That's how I know it's Max, Mama, 'cause of the warm way he feels. And I know he'll always stay with me and be my best friend.

When Daddy comes home he gets a can of beer and starts to drink, and then he sees my kitty. He says, What the hell is that? Only he doesn't sound too mad. And I say, I found him, Daddy. His feet look like he has white socks on. And Daddy says, Put it back where you found it. Only he says it so light I can hardly hear. I say, What

Daddy? Get rid of it! He pulls a bag of potato chips out of the cupboard. We can't have a kitten here, he says. It's not allowed. My heart squeezes up inside me and I say, Please, Daddy, he's my friend. I could hide him and he wouldn't bother anybody. Daddy sits down at the kitchen table and tears open the bag of chips and pours them out on the table. After a drink of beer, he burps real loud and then he looks at me. Okay, he says, 'cause I'm not going to let that nosy manager make all the rules around here. You can feed the cat out on the steps. But he can't come inside here ever again.

Oh, Daddy, I say, not even to sleep with us? At night? When no one can see? Daddy shakes his head and his eyes are almost closed. Never, kid. It'll be an outside cat or no cat at all. Take it or leave it. I say, He'll run away from us, Daddy. He laughs real hard then. Not a chance, not if you feed him. This beats garbage cans all to hell. And I say, Can I play with him outside? When I say so, Daddy says. And only when I'm home. Will he still be mine, Daddy? He shrugs his shoulders at me. Sure, for as long as you feed him. But you'd better do what I tell you. If I ever catch that cat here again—He gives me a bad look and I know what it means. I say, All right, Daddy, and then he says, Now! He raises up his thumb and jerks it at the door. Out! I put the dish of milk and Max outside, and I can tell the sun is starting to go down. Can I stay out a while, Daddy? I'm telling you, kid, he won't go away. And even if he does, he'll be back. Now get in here.

Only I'm worried about Max. What if it rains, Daddy? He gets up and pulls my arm and makes me come inside. So what if it does? He's been wet before. Then Daddy sits down and makes me get on his lap. Are you going to ignore me now that you have a cat? I say no and his arms are sweating around me and he smells bad. Don't I even get a kiss now? he says. I pull off him a little, and his hand gets tight on my arm right where some kitty scratches are. So I raise my face up to him, but he doesn't kiss me. He pulls me closer and I can feel his hand on different places of me, moving fast—like the way the nightmonster does. And then Daddy makes a big burp and says, Later, and he pushes me off him and gets up.

When I'm in bed, Mama, and I can hear it's raining and it's all dark and Daddy is gone away, I start to worry about Max again. I go to the front door and open it to see if he's there. Only I don't see him, so I start calling, Maxie, Maxie, and I wait a long time but he doesn't come. And I want to cry 'cause I think Max will never come back and maybe something has hurt him in the night. But then I hear this tiny sound and Max walks right up to me, only he's all wet. I bring him in the kitchen and dry him off with the dish towel. Then I bring him to bed with me and we talk. It *is* Max 'cause he tells me so and he puts his nose right up to mine and says, I love you. And I ask him where you are, Mama, but he says he doesn't know. Then he crawls off the bed and I can't see him anymore.

Pretty soon I think of a way to make him come back to me. I get some milk and put it in a dish, and Max comes right up to me and starts to drink it. I quess he's been hungry for a long, long time. Then I hear Daddy coming up the stairs, and I turn off the light real quick and take Max into the bedroom. I put him right in the closet, and I jump into bed and play like I'm asleep. Daddy sits down on the bed and starts to take off his shoes, and I can tell he's mad because of the way he's talking to himself. My heart goes so fast I'm scared it will jump out of me, and then Daddy gets into bed. Only I can tell he isn't sleepy 'cause he doesn't move one bit. And then I hear something. It's Maxie. He's crying to get out.

Daddy sits straight up in bed. He says, What the hell is that? I open my eyes. Daddy snaps on the light and looks at me real surprised. Is that goddamned animal in here? *Is he?* I open my mouth, but Daddy raises up his finger and shakes it at me. Don't you dare lie! I say, I'm sorry, Daddy. He gets up real fast and says, Where is he? I'm shaking as I slide down off the bed. I'll get him Daddy. I go to the closet. In there? Daddy yells. Peeing in my shoes maybe? Or worse? I open the door and Max comes running out like he's been waiting for the chance and Daddy goes right after him. I'm screaming, Don't! And Daddy turns back to me and his face is all red and he says, Shut up. One more noise out of you and I'll smash you against the fucking wall!

He chases my kitty around the apartment and the more he tries to catch Max, the madder he gets 'cause he can't do it. And I just keep hoping Max will get away. 'Cause I know what will happen if Daddy catches him and I'm turning all cold inside like a stone. And I keep thinking, Hide, Maxie, hide! Then I hear him squeal and Daddy is standing in the doorway and my kitty is there squirming in his hands. Look, Daddy says to me and he's waving Max back and forth in the air. And he says, Come here, Carla. Come with me.

I follow him into the kitchen and make my fingernails hurt the insides of my hands. Why did you do it? says Daddy. I watch him put Max down on the table, but Daddy still keeps holding onto him, mostly on the neck. It was raining, Daddy. He got all wet. Daddy lifts up my kitty and slams him back down on the table and Max is screaming. I told you cats are waterproof, Daddy says. I'm sorry, Daddy. It was all my fault. And now there's this funny gray color in front of my eyes.

You didn't believe me, Carla, and you didn't mind me either. Daddy's voice is getting quieter and I don't like that. I told you what would happen, he says. My mind is empty. Then he says in a different voice, He is a little wet, Carla. What should we do? Max isn't fighting him very hard now and I think maybe he is hurt. Answer me! yells Daddy. And I say, Dry him off, only I know it doesn't matter now. I know it's too late. That's no good, Daddy says, and his eyes are looking all around now, but he's still holding on tight to Max and Max moves just a little bit and I know it's hard for him to breathe.

Then suddenly Max gets away some and fights real hard and scratches Daddy and I wish he could grow great big, as big as the nightmonster, so he could kill my daddy. But Daddy doesn't even notice Max is scratching him. If we had a dryer, Daddy says, and he seems like he's thinking hard, we could put him in there. He looks around the kitchen again and says, When I was little my mother used to dry our clothes on the clothesline. Then his words start to get faster and faster. But sometimes the socks didn't dry enough so she'd put them in the oven for a while. Daddy looks at our stove and he looks right at the door of the oven and he smiles. Maybe his little socks are still wet, Carla. What do you think? And, Mama, he brings Max over to me then and puts him right in my arms. My kitty feels so light and he's moving just a little bit.

You hold him, Carla, while I light the pilot. Daddy turns his back to me and kneels down on the floor and gets a match out of his pocket and lights the stove. My hands are shaking too much to pet Max and I look at the back door and I know I have to run. Only how can I get away without my Daddy knowing it? And catching us? I look at my Daddy's back and I think about Hansel and Gretel. If only I was strong enough I could push him into the oven. But even if I was strong enough, Mama, he's too big. He's way too big.

I hear the pilot light go on and Daddy closes the oven door. We have to let it get nice and warm in there, he says. He goes to the fridge and gets out a bottle and puts it on the table. He watches me holding Max and he is smiling that bad smile. Please don't hurt him, Daddy. It was all my fault. He smiles more. You know, that's right. It wasn't his fault. It was you who didn't mind. I tell you what—I'll make a deal with you. A hoping feeling comes up inside me. What, Daddy? He takes a drink out of the bottle and wipes his lips. You can take your kitty's place in there.

After he says that I can't stop looking at him, Mama. I'm scared 'cause the oven's getting real hot. I can feel it some and so can Max. That's only fair, says Daddy, isn't it? He is smiling and he puts his hand on my kitty's tail in this nice way. Well? he says. I think it would be all right to die, Mama, but I'm scared of that oven. And what if I didn't die? What if I get burned and then he makes me come out again? One of you is going in there, says Daddy, and his voice is mean and hard this time. Which is it?

Max is moving on me. I love you Carla, he says to me. I love you so much I'll die for you. No, not die, I think. And I say, Daddy, you wouldn't let Max die in there? And Daddy says, What did you call him? And then I know I made a bad mistake. What did I tell you about that name? And Daddy is yelling. And I say, Not to ever say it, Daddy. Not even *think* it! Daddy makes his hand into a fist and pounds on the table. I told you to forget about that kid, Carla. That little bastard. But you don't because you're really a bad girl. And you're going to be punished. Please, Daddy, no—I'll be good. I'll mind you always and always.

But he has the bad smile again. Damn right. Now answer me. Which one of you goes in that oven? I look down and see that one of my kitty's legs is all crooked. I'll do it, Max tells me. I want to. I lift Max up and look right at my Daddy. The kitten it is then, says Daddy, and he is still smiling. He comes over and takes Max away from my hands and opens the oven door and the hot air comes out to us. My body gets all still and Daddy says, Tell Max good-bye. I try to say good-bye but I can't hear me say it. When Daddy closes the oven door, I hear Max screaming.

We must keep our house in order, Daddy says. Then Daddy opens his mouth and he is laughing. And Mama, I have to go to the dark place inside me, the Not-There Place where nothing moves in me. My eyes get sore 'cause they don't blink and I'm looking at the faucet and I can see it dripping. I keep looking at it till everything gets quiet and I know Max is asleep. Then I know how much I want to be with him. I want to go to sleep in the oven, too. I tell Daddy but he says, You made your choice, Carla. You killed him. He kneels down and opens up the oven door and that's when I know for sure it really happened.

I'm bad, Mama. I am always bad.

And I hate everything.

When I open my eyes, Jessie, pieces of my life are spread out obscenely on the desk before me—the notes I have written.

I find I cannot stay in his office now.

I pass through the kitchen, taking a paring knife from the drawer as I go.

In the little bathroom off the front hall, I switch on the light and look at my reflection there.

It is the beginning of the horror.

My head, and my hair so short and light you can hardly see it, and my pale featureless face and the dark ugly bruises on my neck—I look at them all together and see something in the mirror I have never seen before.

My head, rising up from my engorged neck and shoulders—it is monstrous.

I am throwing up in the toilet.

I go back to look again and this time the horror is more real. It is not only the head now, but the head and the neck together, as one.

I am ill. I am mad. Because I can't pull away from that loathesome image, that vile protrusion, with its sickly mottled skin, coming straight up out of my scrawny shoulders.

Then I can see the nightmonster's face as big as the whole ocean and the way he is laughing and getting closer, and I scream out, *"Don't come!"* But I can't help it that he wants me and must have me, that he opens his great mouth to devour me.

Because I am the loggie.

I am the poisoned source.

There is only one answer now. I see myself lift the small knife up beside my head, and as I draw the blade down my temple and cheek, a thrill passes through me. I feel no pain.

With relief I watch the slow steady formation of blood in the wound, and I am satisfied.

Mymouse:	There's blood in the house.
	There's blood on Mymouse.
Punkey:	I'll cut off his head
	And the king will be dead!
Leona Ly:	It's too late to forgive
	He has no right to live.
Kristal:	Build a fire—build a fire
	For his funeral pyre.

It will soon be light out. I should be tired, but I'm not.

Truth seems to be the ultimate stimulation. And I have drunk deeply tonight.

I am free now to do what I must.

To face him.

And to blind him with my sun.

If only I could touch you, Jessie—even once.

But I am like Emily, lacking in courage while alive. Still I have made a pact with the truth, and my letters will always be waiting.

Please don't forget me, my Jessie.

Hold me gently in your hands.

Six

_____

YOU STIR IN YOUR SLEEP, *my father. Sunlight pours wantonly into the room and your eyes will soon open. Patiently enduring the stale reek of you, I wait, your gun alert once again in my hands.*

Two final charges remain in your bill of indictment.

Theft.

And murder.

The stealing of a child from her mother's arms.

The merciless termination of all hope.

You yawn deeply. And again. I see the movement of that big hand as it scratches your knee. I watch you as you instinctively fondle your private parts.

I am here, my father, waiting for you. My face brazenly disfigured now. The die cast.

And I am waiting for your smile. That sweet smile as familiar to me as the morning sun.

But instead, with a grimace, you pull yourself up and grab, more purposefully this time, at your genitals. Your feet touch the floor. And I know your intention as surely as if it were my own bladder.

I am admirably composed. "No," I tell you. "Don't move."

Your are rubbing your eyes. When you finally focus them on me, you breathe, "Jesus, what happened to your face?"

I am sitting up very straight now and I raise the gun just a little so you can see it. "Stay on the bed."

You are reaching out to me with one hand, while the other remains at your crotch. "Give that thing here!"

I can imagine the beginning rush of adrenaline in your body. Powerful now, I can observe. "No, Dad. I have something to tell you."

You stand up.

I feel the instant distortion of my own face, the tightening of my lips in bitter resolution as I swing up the gun. When I speak, my voice has an unusual timbre: "I would love to kill you now."

You sit down on the bed again, your mouth gaping open in confusion.

And I say, "Not one word. Or you'll die."

You have become a statue, your face a bloodless mask, your hands seeking refuge in your lap. And after a second it comes: the singular odor of fresh urine.

I am breathing now from deep inside, and I say, "I can remember that place far away when I was little. The trees standing all aflame on carpets of gold. And how the birds sounded when my own heart beat fast like theirs. And as joyously, as freely. I remember Broder behind me in the sled and the two of us soaring down the hill together, diamond flakes of snow flying past us in the cold, pure air. I remember going inside at dusk for Mama's wonderful chocolate and the story of the little princess."

Bewilderment enlivens your bloodshot eyes; silent pleading softens your broad, pale face.

"Beautiful things I remember, Dad. Almost Perfect Things. The way Mama would kiss me on the end of my nose after she dressed me. And sing songs I didn't understand and cry sometimes. Hold me close and whisper: 'Carlek means love.' "

Your tears are beginning now, my father, spilling out plaintively as a child's do.

And I say, "But then it changed. Everything."

No—don't look away from me, my father. Not now, for you don't dare. My breath is coming short and fast as I look at you. My heart beats freely. "The night-monster came into my life. He made ugly, hurtful places on my Mama's body. And then he put his monster hands on me."

I am aware that you are coming nearer, shifting your body in that stealthy way along the bed. And I am relieved, my father. It is most fitting that you come to me for this—the first and only act of love between us.

I am looking at your chest, implacable and bare as it moves toward me now, and my breathing slows again.

In the beginning was the word. Your word, my father. Impalpable as air and, for me, as necessary. Yet quite meaningless to you.

You are very near. At this moment I can see everything in your sad, tired eyes. And, as my brain summons all the will I have left, you say it—the last of the forbidden words: "Carla."

Now, Daddy—now!

The very sound of the shot is an assault jolting me backward. And then the stillness.

After a time I feel something warm and heavy on my legs.

It is your head, where you've fallen forward at my feet.

I rise and gently free myself. Then I lay the gun down on your chair.

You are silent now, my father. I can smell your blood, but I do not look at you at all. I am calm. I am strong. As I leave your room, I close the door softly. And with respect.

I move through the strange silent house to my room. I wrap myself in my old quilt.

And now I lay me down to sleep.

As soon as I close my eyes I feel her soft arms around me, her tears warm on my skin. . . .

Oh, Mama, please don't cry.

Don't be afraid anymore.

I'm here. And I will keep you safe forever and forever.

It's over now. All over.

The seal is broken.